Lady Mary Contrary

Lady Mary Contrary

Regency Ever After Book 2

A historical romance by
ANNEKA WALKER

OTHER BOOKS BY ANNEKA WALKER
Love in Disguise
The Masked Baron

Regency Ever After Series:
Her Three Suitors (book 1)

Cover design by Blue Water Books
Vintage scroll clipart 33991" is used courtesy of Clipartroo.com

First Printing: January 2020

ISBN:

To Emily

My cheerleader, writing partner, and dear friend

Acknowledgements

Going from manuscript to print takes more than just one little writer. I need to thank all those on my writer team! Thank you, Shaela, for a wonderful cover. Summer, you did a fantastic job with your edits! Emily, you always give me the best reactions and story advice. Kaylie, your guidance inspired the last chapter. Heather, your eye for detail is so appreciated. Sally, thank you for sharing your advice with me. My husband, Jonathan, deserves lots of thanks for his continual patience and constant encouragement. And, most of all, I want to thank my Heavenly Father. He is the giver of all things. Every story He grants me is a blessing and a learning experience.

Mary, Mary, quite contrary,
How does your garden grow?
With silver bells, and cockleshells,
And pretty maids all in a row

Chapter One

Banbury Castle, Oxfordshire, England, 1803

Mary pulled back the damask curtain in the alcove on the second floor and saw a carriage come up the drive. She knelt on her chair for a better view, pushing her collection of seashells to one side of the window ledge to make room for her elbow, and held her breath. Her eldest brother Anton stepped out first and then Terrance, the brother just older than her. Anton put out his hand and helped their mother down. The carriage door shut behind them and finally, Mary's breath released. No one else followed.

They'd dropped *him* off before returning home. Good riddance.

Blake—Mr. Gunther now that they were no longer children—had left with her brothers to win the fair heart of the most exquisitely beautiful woman Mary had ever seen. And now she would learn who had won. One of her brothers, or Blake.

Mary squeezed past the metal knight statue that blocked her secret place of reprieve, and smoothed her cornflower-blue morning dress. She took a bracing breath and forced herself to walk down the stairs to greet her family. Why did it feel like she was marching to her own execution?

It was easy to predict who the victor would be. Anton might be an earl now, but he could be awkward around the opposite gender, and Terrance had no desire to marry for several years to come. She also knew Blake to be the most handsome man she had ever laid eyes on. He could charm a snake. Mary wished she could say she was immune to him.

Their butler, Pearl, pulled open the door as she reached the last stair. In walked her mother, escorted by Anton. Her eyes went straight to Anton's depressed features. Mary felt a little faint. No matter how she tried to prepare herself, she could not bear to hear the outcome of their house party.

"Mary, dear!" Mother put out her arms and Mary rushed into them.

She needed this comfort, ached for it. "I'm ever so glad you're home." Mary burrowed her head into her mother's shoulder.

"Good heavens! What is the matter?"

Mary pulled back and did her best to keep the moisture in her eyes from spilling over. No matter how many times her tears wet her pillow, there seemed to be more the next day. She wiped her cheeks dry and forced a smile. "I've missed you is all. How is my sister? And how is the new baby?"

"Jillian is exhausted. Baby June is darling. And I would not be surprised if their nursemaid does not bring the rest of her children here within the fortnight. I told Jillian to send them with me, but she would not be parted from them."

Mary frowned. "Oh dear. That doesn't sound good."

"No," her mother answered. "You know how stubborn your sister is. Her health is vastly more important than a few weeks without her older children."

"But how did you arrive home in the same carriage as my brothers?"

"They stopped to see the baby on their way home from visiting Rosewood Park. So here I am."

Anton cleared his throat. "Well, if no one has a hug for their favorite brother, I shall just be off then."

Mary turned to her generally serious brother and couldn't help but try to tease a smile. "Of course I have a hug for Terrance. Where is he?"

Terrance came up behind Anton. Since Terrance was taller, his amused expression could not be hidden. "Did someone say my name?"

Anton groaned. "Very well. Every woman seems to favor him. Why should you be no different?"

Mary spread her arms and leapt towards Anton before he could step away. She knew he must be heartbroken—she felt the same unrequited love towards Blake—and she longed to comfort her brother.

"I'm only teasing." She pulled back and narrowed her eyes. "You know I love you and Terrance the exact same. Which hardly means anything since I am still angry you left me in the first place."

"You didn't miss anything," Anton huffed.

"Was it so very awful?" Mary could only imagine Miss Bliss rolling her eyes at her brothers' attempts to woo her.

Terrance stepped forward and put his arm around Mary. "Not so very terrible as all that." He grinned at her like he'd escaped the misery of falling for Miss Bliss unlike everyone else.

Mary leaned into him, happy to have her family home at last. "You can say that Terrance, only because you left without any intention of winning over any hearts."

"He is the one who conquered," Anton said with a sigh, "where Gunther and I did not."

Mary blanched. "Wait, what does this mean?" She needed someone to spell it out for her.

Anton pointed to Terrance. "He's engaged to be married."

Pulling out of Terrance's arm, Mary stared at him. "You? But…" she sputtered. "You told me you did not intend to marry. How did this happen?"

Terrance shrugged. "Generally, a man asks a woman to marry her, and then the lady says either yes or no. In this case, she said yes."

"She chose *you*?" Mary put her hands to her temples.

Terrance rolled his eyes. "If you will not believe me, then who shall?"

Realizing she'd hurt Terrance's feelings, she dropped her hands. "Forgive me. You are just as handsome as Anton and Blake."

"Mr. Gunther," her mother corrected, after handing Pearl her hat. While Mother was an unusually tenderhearted countess, she spent a great deal of time attempting to train her children in the formalities of society. "You are not children. How many times must I remind you?"

"Please, Mother. Mary was just telling me how handsome I am." Terrance grinned at Mary. "Go ahead."

Mary looked at the ceiling with mock exasperation. "I will let your intended stroke your ego. I am only surprised because I thought your intent lay elsewhere. I am happy for you." In truth, she was a little dizzy. "When is the wedding?"

Terrance tapped his chin as he thought. "Seven weeks, six days, and three hours."

"Utterly maddening," Anton said, stalking off. "Send him away so we shall have peace until then."

Mary and Terrance watched him leave.

"Anton may never forgive me," Terrance whispered. His tone held true sorrow.

"Give him time," Mary said, reaching for his arm. "He did not love her, just the idea of her."

"Yes, well, tell that to Gunther too."

Mary did not even want to know how crushed Blake was. Even as she thought it, she started trying to imagine the answer. Was he heartbroken? She shook her head. The man was an idiot. Why should she care if he nursed a heartache? He deserved worse.

"Why the scowl?" Terrance asked. "You think Gunther will hate me forever too?"

Mary lifted her gaze back to meet Terrance's. "I hope he does. I hope he stays as far away from you and this family as the plague. I hope Blake . . ."

"Mr. Gunther," her mother corrected, popping her head out from the drawing room door before disappearing again.

Mary made an unladylike grunt and folded her arms across her chest.

"What is it with you two?" Terrance asked, real concern on his face.

How to explain? With her heart safe a little longer, now all she could feel was anger. "All you need to know is that if the house is burning down and only *Mr. Gunther* and a sack of rotten potatoes are left inside, I'm going to save the potatoes!"

Mary spun around and marched back up the stairs. It didn't matter if Blake was still unattached. Perhaps deep, deep inside she could admit to a touch of relief he did not marry so soon after . . . well, it didn't matter. With no more reason to cry over the man, now she could just focus on her anger. At least her brothers had the sense to leave Blake at his home and not bring him here.

The last thing she wanted was to ever, ever see the man again. She stomped into her room and shut the door with a little too much force. She pulled out a piece of paper and sat at her desk. With her drawing pencils, she sketched a rough image. First the eyes. Blake's eyes were dark, deceiving her that those pools of brown could see into her soul. She drew his nose, this time without the accuracy she'd given his eyes. She extended the nose making it long and bulbous. His smile came next — his wickedly, corrupt lips. She made his teeth long in front and added his signature dimples. She sighed. Those beautiful dimples. Her eyes hardened as she scribbled away at his blond hair. The man thought he had the hair of Adonis the way he fluffed it constantly.

Blake Gunther was a conceited cow.

When she finished, she stood and walked to a picture on the wall depicting Banbury Castle, her home. She'd sketched it and father had framed it for her. She pulled it down and stabbed Blake's portrait onto the nail. There. Now she only required a few darts to throw at it. Or rocks. Whichever she could find first. She put the frame on the desk and grabbed her shawl for a walk. A bit of fresh air and some harmless entertainment would rid her heart of the only man she had ever loved.

Chapter Two

Blake Gunther might go mad. His own mother sat before him with cold accusations on her tongue. There was not an ounce of doting sympathy for his recent broken heart. Convinced of his rogue behavior — heartless, indulgent, and without morals — Blake might as well have been an advocate of the devil.

"My son, my own flesh and blood, is a vile sinner."

Blake resisted rolling his eyes and appealed to his mother's sensibilities. Sure, Blake enjoyed harmless flirtations, but nothing untoward. "The neighbors are simply jealous. Their sons do not come from handsome stock like me. It is to your own credit, you know. Have some pride in your offspring."

His mother threw her head in her hands and began to weep. "My son is an adulterer!"

Blake's eyes bulged and his mouth unhinged. He knew of a rumor or two with his name attached, but this was a bit thick. He turned to his father. His, dear, useless father. Never had he known a man more spineless. His father gave him a commiserating glance and then went back to his beetle collection.

Sometimes Blake thought he must have been adopted from some unknown family. He was nothing like his parents in personality. However, he had the same broad shoulders of his mother and the same blond hair and stormy eyes as his much shorter father. Blake did love them both dearly, even if he could not understand them.

He leaned forward and handed his mother a handkerchief. She accepted it, mopped up her face, and blew her nose like a trumpet.

"There, there, Mother. Do not upset yourself needlessly."

His mother's eyes jumped to his. "No? While you were away at a house party, your father and I were subject to a visit from three different people, including the vicar. Each had a story and bade us to caution you before more young ladies suffered at your hand."

Blake sat back and the stiff wooden chair in their library creaked as if it might snap under his weight. He was not a small man. He had won many rounds in the pugilist ring in college but turned a spectator when he realized the importance of keeping his face unmarred and all his teeth — two important things for a bachelor.

"Everyone steals a kiss now and then," Blake petitioned, "but I promise I am a gentleman, and you do not have any reason to be disappointed in me."

"Stealing kisses?" His mother gasped, and she nearly knocked her lacy mobcap from her head as she flung her hand to her forehead. "Mr. Gunther? Mr. Gunther?"

"Yes, dear?" his father asked, holding a large magnifying glass up to his latest acquired sample.

"Did you hear what he said?"

"I did," his father answered, completely uninterested.

"I am afraid there is only one course of action." His mother took a deep breath to calm her nerves and then offered his death sentence. "I'm cutting you off until you marry. You can have your horse, but if you travel farther than twenty miles, I will see he is gone too."

Blake gripped the chair so hard the arm fell off. He turned to secure it back. He should never have returned home. At least he could go to his friend's house a few miles away. He'd spent most of his youth there avoiding his unhinged family.

Blake turned back to his parents. "Surely, you cannot be serious. You can trust that I am who I say I am. When have I ever disappointed you? Hmm?"

His mother's brow raised. "When you were eight and broke the window in the garden shed. When you were ten and cut off the braid of Lady Mary. When you were fourteen and put your father's beetle collection on the cake we served the vicar. When you were fifteen and scared the children at the cemetery. When you were seventeen and I received a letter from school of your repeated nighttime wanderings. Need I go on? I think I could entertain us both for several days with my recounting. The point is, you have gone too far this time."

His mother generally exaggerated, but her list of his misdeeds was painfully and entirely accurate. He did not esteem himself as much of a troublemaker until she painted his character so perfectly. Now even *he* wondered.

"No money?"

"Not a farthing."

Blake swallowed back the breakfast that threatened to make an ugly appearance. That meant no leaving town. That meant living with his parents, possibly until his father died and he received his inheritance. He looked at his father. The man was healthier than most his age. He spent most of his time out of doors exercising as he searched for his bugs.

A sigh escaped his mouth, and he found himself humbly agreeing to the situation presented to him. What was his choice? The cards were stacked against him. His father would never be persuaded to argue with his wife. And his mother, an ostentatiously stubborn woman, had him pegged as a philanderer.

Blake excused himself and made his way to the stables. A bruising ride would do him good. A stable boy brought out Stargazer, his handsome Arabian blood horse. Was it a crime if Blake possessed nice things? Would someone slander his name because of his horse too? He wished he had the names of his accusers. The vicar never liked him, so no surprise there. But who were the others that threw his name under the cart?

He mounted his horse and urged him into a run. The countryside around his home soothed him as nothing else could. He did look forward to coming home, but this — the trees, the open space, the clean air — this is what pulled him there every summer, not the stone and mortar. His younger sisters were fun to tease, but there was a decade gap between them in age. Thankfully, his best friends were like his brothers and treated him as one of their family. He could see Banbury Castle as Stargazer's long strides narrowed the distance.

The castle had belonged to the earl's family for only a few generations and had been rebuilt to outwardly resemble the medieval fortress it had once been. The enclosed courtyard in its gray, boxlike shape with menacing brattices might not seem welcoming to some, but what was left of the moat and the defensive border wall provided hours of playtime for a couple of boisterous boys. Blake did not even realize he'd intended on visiting today. The route was habitual after all these years.

Stargazer loped across the Banbury Bridge, past the market place, and around the back of the castle toward the stables. Blake was sweating when he pulled Stargazer to a stop — worse than his horse. He gave the reins over to Lord Crawford's stable hand and stalked off toward the gardens. Now that he was here, he didn't care to see or talk to anyone. Anton would commiserate with him, and Terrance, well, Terrance would be pining for his sweet fiancé. The girl he stole from Blake.

"You!"

Blake whipped his head around, surprised to see Mary behind him, walking near a small orchard. Well, it was Lady Mary now, but since she had always been simply Mary since they were children, it seemed difficult to call her anything else.

"You!" she repeated. "You dare come here?"

Her enchanting blue eyes and gleaming black hair were a trick of the light. She was far from an angel. Most thought him an affable fellow, unless they asked his mother. But Mary either hated him or she was his dearest confidante. Never in between.

Blake doffed his hat and bowed. "Lady Mary, how ravishing you look. Might you accept my arm, and the two of us can experience a romantic stroll through the trees?"

Her eyes narrowed, shooting sparks his way.

"I'm jesting, Mary. Come on."

"*Lady* Mary."

Blake shook his head and grinned. "I meant no disrespect. You're simply too easy to tease when you're angry with me." In truth, Mary scared him when she was angry. It was all he could do to try to change her mood. "Let us begin anew. How did you spend the last month?"

Mary's eyes seemed to glower even more. Her month could not have been as horrible as his.

"Was it lonely without your mother and brothers?"

Mary turned away from him and folded her arms across her chest. "You may go now. You are not welcome here."

Blake stretched his back and arms while she was turned away. Their crowded carriage ride from Rosewood Park still haunted him. "Listen, you were angry with me when we all left London for Rosewood Park. I can't explain it for the life of me. Perhaps you can spare me the guessing game and just tell me, so I might apologize."

Mary stood there with her back to him, not backing down an inch. She reminded him of Mary's older sister, Jillian. But even more so, she reminded him of their Irish grandmother — a widow as stubborn as a mule and as fiery as a blazing hot furnace. Thankfully, that trait only fell to the women in the family and spared his best friends.

"Don't you even want to hear about our trip?" What he wanted to do was vent to Mary about his mother. He remembered many hours spent talking in the past, but now that they were grown up, everything felt so different.

"I already heard about the trip from my brothers. You and Anton lost and Terrance won. And you shan't have any sympathy from me." Mary turned slowly in his direction. Her face was still guarded, but at least she was speaking to him. "And it isn't proper for you to be out here when I am, and I was here first."

Blake clenched his jaw. "Very well, you stay here, and I will walk in the other direction." He gave her a flourishing bow and stalked off toward the house. Where could he go where he wasn't looked at as a hindrance to the world?

"Gunther!" Anton called, crossing the yard toward him with a dog prancing around him for attention. "Didn't we just get rid of you?"

Blake pushed his jacket back and rested a hand on his hip. He couldn't even take a little barb. He was feeling just a tiny bit sensitive. "It looks as if you should suffer my company forever."

"Your mother again?"

"Who else?"

"My sister tends to give your mother a run, doesn't she?" He motioned his head toward Mary's form now disappearing into the distant trees.

Blake hated to agree with him. "I could pass around a petition against myself and I should think the entire community would sign it. I don't know why you tolerate my company at all."

"I don't," Anton joked. "But I prefer you to my brother just now."

Blake looked at the weary face of his friend and cringed. "You are taking the jilting of Miss Bliss harder than I."

"I do not think you imagined yourself marrying her."

Blake raised a brow. "No, no I did not. I certainly had my head turned, but I'm not the settling down type. I'm just not ready." He thought of his mother's threats and shivered. He could marry and lose his freedom or not marry and lose his freedom. Either way, he was doomed.

"Yes, it is fortunate your father is alive and you have no reason to be settled."

Blake grimaced. Anton had it much worse than he. "We have been over this time and time again. You attract the wrong sort when you are desperate. Take your time. Things will come when they should."

If only Blake had such a luxury! He could not impose on Anton and his family for the duration of the summer. Especially with Anton depressed, Mary despising him, and Terrance gloating over winning the hand of the prettiest girl in all of England. No, he needed money to leave when he wished. And even though he'd been home for less than half an hour, he felt stifled already.

Chapter Three

Mary found Terrance in his room, no doubt penning a letter to Miss Bliss. She knocked on the open door to capture his attention. He peered over his shoulder at her and raised his eyebrows expectantly.

"Are you terribly busy? I just need a minute." Terrance had always been her closest sibling.

Terrance turned in his seat and stretched out his long legs. "I will be generous and give you two minutes. What is it?"

Mary stepped into the room and pulled the door shut behind her.

"Ah? Something secret then?"

Mary sighed. "I need your help."

"Let me guess? Gunther?"

Mary met his eyes. "How did you know?"

"Everyone knows you care for him, Mary. You would have to be blind, deaf, and live in a hole in the ground to miss it. You don't exactly hide your feelings very well."

Mary squirmed. "I cannot be that bad."

"Worse," Terrance said.

She sighed. "Well then help me fix this. You won over Miss Bliss when no one else could. Help me."

"How? You want me to shoot Gunther in the foot so he won't keep coming here? Or do you want me to tie him up and force him to ask for your hand in marriage?"

Mary scrunched up her nose. "Neither will do. If he cannot fix this himself, then he needs a slice of humble pie. I am quite vexed with him."

"You are always angry with Gunther."

Mary swallowed back her emotions. "I know. What can be done, Terry?"

Terrance leaned forward over his knees and clasped his hands together, his hazel eyes considering her question. "You need to decide if you want things to work out or not."

"After everything, how could I want them to work out?"

"Can you never forgive him?"

Mary shook her head. "Never."

"Then could you learn to live without him?"

A tear escaped. "Never."

Terrance groaned. "Mary Contrary, here we go again."

"Stop! I hate that nickname!"

"Listen. I want you to be happy. Blake Gunther is my best friend. But is he capable of being everything you deserve?"

Mary wiped at her eyes. "Can I figure it out later? I require a small favor first."

"Depends on the favor."

"Might you invite over a handsome bachelor friend for dinner? With Blake in attendance, of course."

"Mr. Gunther," Terrance corrected.

Mary rolled her eyes. "Fine. Mr. Gunther."

Terrance studied her for a moment. "I'll do it, but it will be up to you to do the rest."

His agreement melted her frown. "I will. I love you, Terry."

Terrance turned back to face his letter. "Just don't be too free with your affection. The rest of your life depends upon it."

Mary gave him an offended glare. "I am not a strumpet. You can trust that."

"I'm simply cautioning you from loving the first person who offers for you just because he isn't Gunther. I want you to marry a man who deserves you." He pinned her with a very sincere look.

Mary pulled the door open, wishing Gunther could deserve her, or even desire to deserve her. "I'll do my very best."

"Lord Templeton, might I introduce my daughter?" Mother asked, directing him to Mary. "This is Lady Mary, my youngest."

Lord Templeton could not have been more distinguished. He bore a double-knotted cravat, and his pin-striped gray waistcoat and black dinner jacket only enhanced his dark features. Long eyelashes accentuated his deep brown eyes and his dark curls were styled in a trim, Roman cut.

He took Mary's hand and bowed over it. "There is not a soul in the neighborhood I've met who has not boasted about the charms of the new Banbury Castle. I see it is *you* they were speaking of, not the house."

A pleasant warmth spread through her. Terrance had outdone himself with this man. He was everything—rich, titled, handsome, and even appeared to be sincere.

"You are too generous in your compliments. When you see more of Banbury Castle, you will see the neighborhood was right." Mary wanted to say something witty, but she was too busy admiring how perfect Lord Templeton would be in his role as a suitor. That is, perfect enough to drive Blake mad.

Thinking of Blake seemed to prompt his arrival. He strode into the room and kissed Mary's mother on the cheek like one of her sons. He turned to take Mary's hand and froze. His eyes landed on Lord Templeton, standing very near her, and his eyes narrowed.

"I seem to be in need of an introduction," Blake said, almost caustically.

"This is Lord Templeton," Terrance offered. "He's purchased the Newcliff estate as a summer house."

"Newcliff?" It seemed Blake didn't even know it was for sale.

Anton stepped in beside him. "When Mr. Pierce died, his son felt a more fashionable house elsewhere would suit him better. I daresay, Lord Templeton was the smarter of the two. Newcliff is a jewel."

"I agree," Lord Templeton said. "Except it is a little too quiet for my liking. But when I marry and have a family to fill the walls, I think it should be everything I hope it to be."

"Marry?" Blake asked. "Have you a bride in mind?"

Lord Templeton looked at Mary. "Not yet."

Blake audibly cleared his throat. "Is dinner late?"

The countess put her hand on Blake's shoulder. "Dinner is exactly on time."

There was nothing more pleasing for Mary than striding to dinner with her hand on Lord Templeton's arm, with Blake following behind. She giggled, although from Lord Templeton's quick wit or from the pleasure in her circumstances, Mary could not quite say why.

Chapter Four

Blake's relationship with the Crawford family was unique at best. Not even his mother could complain about the connection, which helped because he preferred dining at Banbury Castle to his own home. It was not unusual to arrive and find the countess had invited other guests. The staff watched for Blake and always set out another place setting for him without bothering to check with the family. Life was predictable in the summers, with the absence of the late Lord Crawford as the only real stark difference in Blake's memory.

Tonight, however, felt different.

Lord Templeton was completely to blame.

Blake observed the way Terrance and even Anton looked to their guest as if he was their superior. What was he? A baron? Anton was an earl for heaven's sake. Blake was a nobody, but that was beside the point.

"We needn't continue to discuss my dreams for Newcliff. I'd hate to bore you on our first evening in company," Lord Templeton said.

"Nonsense," Anton said. "I find your ideas for making your estate more efficient quite fascinating. Is the house staff to your liking? I can't imagine running the staff without a woman's good opinion."

"My judgments are new and perhaps need time to refine. I fear my new butler has an aversion to me. He sneezed on me twice on my way out the door tonight and once yesterday. I'm not sure what to make of it."

The countess laughed. "You are jesting."

"I wish I was. When I return tonight, I am going to hold a handkerchief out as I pass him. It'll save me an unfortunate shower from his nose and him the need to apologize."

"Stop," Mary laughed. "It's too much." Mary was not a demure debutante. When she laughed, it was real. Not too boisterous but thick and rich.

Blake liked to think he was the only one to elicit such laughter—apparently not.

"I daresay, next you will tell us your housekeeper is afraid of you and hides in the cellar," Mary said, leaning toward her guest.

"You have it wrong. It is I who am afraid of her. You think I came here because of your generous invitation, but really I am fleeing a house and staff I have yet to accustom myself to."

"You are welcome here anytime," Lady Crawford said. "My son, Mr. Hadley, is to leave in a few short weeks to his estate in Shropshire to prepare for his new bride. But Lord Crawford and I will gladly keep you company."

"Thank you, your ladyship." Then Lord Templeton turned to Terrance. "Congratulations. I had not heard there were wedding bells in your future."

"The news is as recent as your arrival in the neighborhood." Terrance's smile was one of unabashed happiness. "I consider myself a fortunate man."

Anton's grin fled, and he busied himself with his meal, causing Blake to sigh. He did not value bachelorhood as Blake did, and was clearly still hurting. Why would someone want to marry if it meant a life like his mother's and father's? The idea seemed quite ludicrous to him.

Lord Templeton managed to regale his small audience with stories through dinner and back in the drawing room. His expressions were a mite serious, but he had wit and charm in spades. This was the kind of man Blake might respect, but a different feeling seemed to cramp altogether inside him. He could not define it.

"You're so very wise, Lord Templeton," Mary said, her eyes glued on his.

Blake wanted to gag. Mary had her head turned, and it was almost comical. But it wouldn't last. Mary never cared for another man for long. Her heart was as contrary as she was. Sure, she would express interest, but more as a challenge than anything real. Blake looked closer. This might be different. There was no doubt she was mesmerized by Lord Templeton.

"Any word from Jillian?" Blake asked the countess when her attention seemed to wander from their guest. He needed to stop watching Mary or he'd vomit.

"You know how stubborn my daughter can be," her ladyship said with a sigh. "I am so worried about her and that baby."

Blake agreed. He'd only seen Jillian for a moment on their way home from Rosewood Park, but never had she looked so weak. "I am sure she is commanding everyone to take care of her, and we have no need to fret."

"I am considering returning to offer my help, but I do hate to intrude."

"I don't think that is possible, my lady. You are the least intrusive person I know."

"Thank you, Blake."

Mary suddenly turned to them. "Why would anyone thank him?"

"Mary!" Her mother hushed her. The countess eyed Lord Templeton as if to remind her daughter to mind her manners.

It seemed Lady Crawford hoped Mary would make a good impression on Lord Templeton. Was there some matchmaking going on behind the scenes that he was unaware of?

"I was simply asking after your sister, Lady Mary," Blake said, remembering to address Mary in the proper way. He did try when in company. He was not a complete dolt.

"Oh," Mary said, straightening her posture. "How very kind of you." Then she shifted in her seat to give Lord Templeton her full attention again.

Blake had had enough of her giggles for one night. When dinner ended, he stood and bade everyone goodnight. He needed to come up with a plan for himself, and sitting in the drawing room watching Mary and Lord Templeton was not a scenario to produce quality thought. It meant he would have to return home. To his mother. Perhaps it was time to gather a list of available women in the area. Time for him to consider finding a wife.

Mary giggled again.

He looked back, and a light flickered on in his mind. Mary?

No. She was far above him in beauty and position. Things had not gone so well with the last woman he'd tried to woo, and Mary currently hated him. However, he did know everything there was to know about Mary, and living with her would be vastly better than a life tied to his mother. And he might be doing Mary a favor. Something about Lord Templeton bothered Blake. He was too perfect. Too eager. Mary deserved better than Blake, no doubt, but she didn't deserve to suffer at the hands of a cad either. Blake could be the lesser evil.

Chapter Five

Mary tried reading, but her mind never grasped more than a few pages at a time. She finally dropped her book in her lap and stared at the back of the dingy armor in her tiny alcove. Why did everyone else get lost in stories, while Mary was always lost in her own head? Lord Templeton had been perfect last night; Blake, oddly quiet. Had her new guest made Blake jealous at all?

Then she circled back to Lord Templeton. Lord *Tempting* seemed more fitting. He was everything she wanted in a man: kind, serious, witty, appreciated by all. His position spoke for itself, and he had a house close to Banbury Castle. The situation could not be more ideal.

Of course, if they were to ever marry, she would have to let go of the butler. Mary had no intention of being sneezed on every time she and her husband left the house. Laughing to herself, Mary sunk down in her seat, content to daydream a little longer.

A faint clicking of carriage wheels on their rocky drive caught her attention. Mary turned in her seat and pulled herself up to the window. Her breath caught. Her book fell off her lap as she flew from her seat and squeezed past the armor. Picking up her dress, she hurried down the stairs where Pearl anticipated her and opened the door.

A footman stepped to the carriage door and her nieces piled out.

"Opal! Claire! Gloria!" Mary opened her arms, and the three little girls fell into them. There was no greater joy than being an aunt, and Mary reveled in the responsibility. "What are you doing here?"

Their nursemaid, Hannah, stepped down from the carriage. She was a heavy-set, middle-aged woman with streaks of gray at her temples and distinctive wrinkle lines around her mouth. Everyone adored her, including Mary.

"Lady Jillian is needing some quiet time to recover. She sent us straightway. We didn't stop none, so we might have beat your brother-in-law's letter."

"You know you and the girls are always welcome, Hannah." Mary turned to the footman. "Bring their things to the nursery." Then she stood and swooped little Opal into her arms. "Come girls, your grandmother will be so pleased to see you again."

"I'm hungry," Claire said. "Can we eat here?"

"Yes, dearest," Mary said, reaching for the chubby hand of the dark-haired, always hungry three-year-old. It had been nearly two months since she'd seen the girls, and she was surprised how even baby Opal remembered her. "We shall find Grandmother and the food. Come along."

Pearl opened the door for them, right as Mary's mother swooped down the staircase toward them. She hugged the girls one by one and then ushered them towards the nursery, with Hannah chasing after them.

"Mrs. Grange," her mother said in a hushed tone to the housekeeper, "see they are brought up some lunch."

"Yes, your ladyship." Mrs. Grange said, sharing the countess's worried frown.

"What is it, Mama?" Mary asked. "You expected the children, didn't you?"

"Your sister would never have sent them." Mother brought her hands to her lips. "Jack must have. I fear Jillian is not doing well."

A knock sounded on the door, and Pearl opened it long enough to receive a letter from a messenger.

"Could this be from her?" Mary asked.

Mother took the missive and quickly opened it. Her eyes darted back and forth as she read down to the end.

"It's from Jack. Jillian is not well. He says not to worry yet, but he will send word if she worsens." Mother clutched her dress at her chest. "I can't lose her too."

Mary's heart thudded with her own panic. "Don't be silly, Mama," Mary said, reining in her emotions for her mother's sake. "Jack would have asked you to come if he was at all worried."

"I'm not so sure. Jack does not have the intuition of a mother."

Mary tucked her arm through her mother's. "Perhaps not, but he is intelligent if nothing else. He sent the children to us to allow Jillian to rest. A quiet house is the recipe to her recovery, not unfounded worry." Mary would still worry, but she did not want her mother to.

"How very smart," Blake said from behind her.

Mary looked back and saw Anton and Blake coming in from Anton's study.

"We heard children's voices," Anton said. "What news is there of Jillian?"

"Just that her recovery is taking longer than we hoped."

Anton put his arm around his mother, and Blake went and stood beside Mary.

"How can I be of assistance?" Blake asked, his voice oddly serious for such an usually carefree man.

Mary almost rolled her eyes. "Are you going to offer to go sit with my sister?"

Blake fluffed his hair. "I was thinking more along the lines of charming a few fair-headed young maidens. I expect they are in the nursery?"

Mother nodded. "I would greatly appreciate any time you can spare for the children. Hannah is no doubt exhausted. I am going to have some things packed so I might leave at once if word comes."

"I know what it is to be confined in a carriage for as long as the children have been," Blake said. "I bet they are anxious to run and play. A walk perhaps?"

Mother reached out and covered Blake's hand with her own. "I think that is exactly what they need."

"Claire is hungry," Mary said to Blake, not hiding her annoyance. "I insist on seeing the girls eat before you whisk them outside."

"Very well," Blake said.

"And they must don their coats and bonnets before their walk," Mary added. "With the sky as muted and gray as it is, there will likely be rain."

"Let me know if you need anything, Mama," Anton said. "I have a great deal to catch up on because of my absence."

Mother urged him away. "These two will see to the children. Thank you, Anton."

The last thing Mary wanted to do was volunteer to spend time with Blake, but she wouldn't neglect the children either. "I will make sure Blake does not make things worse, Mama. You can see to your packing."

"Mr. Gunther," Mother reminded her. "And thank you."

"Come, *Mr. Gunther*," Mary said. "I will teach you how to feed a one-year-old."

Blake followed her upstairs. "Certainly. As long as you also see to their nappies. I am only here to provide the entertainment."

Mary glanced at his profile as they walked. Did the man have to be so infuriatingly handsome all the time? It was kind of him to volunteer to take care of the children, but Mary wanted to be the one to do it.

She would have to put aside her harsh feelings for the afternoon. She feared the children would catch onto her mood and worry needlessly. They were already far from their mother and their home. They needed reassurance, not Mary's frustrations. She took a deep breath. She pictured Blake with an apron, making silly faces at the children. If she could keep the image of him as a nursemaid in her mind, then perhaps she would be immune to him.

Chapter Six

Blake watched Mary hurry to help Opal stand again after she'd taken a little spill on the lawn in the courtyard. "There, there, Opal. You're all right."

"Are *you* all right, Mary?" Blake asked. She seemed awfully flustered and for once, he did not think it was because of anything stupid he had said or done.

"Lady Mary," Mary corrected, with a bite to her tone.

Blake groaned. "Forgive me, *my lady*. We both know how impossible it is to be proper in public, but in private it's entirely too much work."

She folded her arms across her chest. "Fine. You can keep calling me Mary. But just while we are with the children."

It was a small victory in overcoming her poor humor, but he would take it. "Are you going to answer my question? There is something bothering you."

"I'm surprised you noticed."

There, the expected jibe. It would be a long, miserable summer if she decided to stay angry with him.

Mary's eyes watched Gloria chase after Claire. "It's Jillian. Do you think anything could happen to her?" Her voice was low, and even the worry sounded like that of a woman, not a child. When did Mary become so grown up? He'd been noticing for some time, but he was still not used to it.

"Your sister was not herself when we visited. I hear childbirth can take a toll on a person."

"I love children," Mary said. She turned to him. "But bearing children sounds so dreadful."

This was the Mary he missed. The one who would confide in him. "You will be brave when the time comes. I know you will."

"I had to keep a good face for Mama, but the truth is, I don't want Jillian to die." Her voice caught.

Blake put his arm out, and Mary came to him. She curled up against him just like the time when her cat had been killed by a carriage wheel. Or more recently, when her dearest friend married and she had felt abandoned. And then there was the horrible night they'd heard the news about Mary's father. This was a familiar position, and yet, thinking of Mary one day turning to someone else — someone like Lord Templeton — made Blake pull her closer. Someday things would change between them, and there would be no looking back. Being adults meant having adult problems, and he knew it was his job to spin the situation into something lighter.

"Do you know what Jillian cares about more than anything?" Blake asked.

"What?" Mary asked, sniffing and batting away a few errant tears.

"These little girls. Let's take good care of them. And then at the end of every day, we will write and tell her about our adventures. You could even send her sketches."

Mary pulled back. "I love your idea. Jillian will likely be worried about them, and the stories will cheer her. We can include drawings from Gloria and Claire, as well as mine."

"And trace Opal's hand for her to see," Blake added.

Mary scrunched her nose. "What will she think of you and I spending so much time together?"

"Because you are supposed to hate me?" Blake asked, curious as to why she would ask such an odd question. Everyone at Banbury Castle spent a lot of time with Blake. It was unavoidable.

Mary nodded. "Precisely. She will think I am weak to have forgiven you already."

"What exactly do you need to forgive me for this time?" Blake asked, stepping much too close and staring down at Mary with wide eyes. "Hmm?" He let his head drop to touch her forehead.

She laughed and pushed him away. "Take your displeasing person over there to watch Opal before she eats that flower. I am going to play princesses with Gloria and Claire, and you will be useless in such a game."

"You deliberately ignored my question again," Blake said, putting his hands on his hips. "And I would make a very fine princess; though, I daresay dragons would be more entertaining."

Mary scoffed. "You might stare at your reflection long enough to qualify as a princess, but you are not going to ruin our fun by adding a dragon. You and Opal run along. My sister is going to have a delightful story today about princesses. I am determined."

Blake loved a good competition. Swooping Opal into his arms before she shoved a flower in her mouth, Blake hurried down to the other two girls, arriving at the same time as Mary.

"Quick, a dragon is coming. Spin in circles as fast as you can to keep him from eating you."

Claire squealed and started spinning. She made it one rotation before she fell down. Blake lifted up Opal and dove toward Claire's stomach. "The dragon is coming!" Claire squealed and rolled away. She stood and started running, only to trip because she was laughing so hard.

"The dragon can't get me," Gloria said.

Blake flew Opal over to Gloria to win her over. Soon peals of laughter emitted from both Opal's and Gloria's mouths. "Spin in circles, Gloria! Spin."

Gloria was soon weaving back and forth from spinning so much. She collapsed with a delighted sigh of pleasure.

Turning, Blake flew Opal toward Mary. "Spin in circles before the dragon eats you."

Mary shook her head. "Oh no. This is not nearly as fun as princesses, I guarantee."

"Uh oh, girls." Blake turned to Gloria and Claire. "Where are my other dragons? Mary isn't spinning in circles? Who will help me eat her?"

"I will!"

"Me, me. I want to be a dragon."

Mary gave him a playful scowl. He swooped Opal up into the air, her little arms swinging with tiny giggles erupting from her mouth. Mary realized he was serious and turned to run. He tucked Opal on his hip and with his other arm, captured Mary around the waist.

"Get her, dragons!"

Gloria and Claire dove at Mary's legs, bowling into them. Mary started to go down but Blake pulled her tight against him.

"That was close," he said, although his words seemed literal now since Mary's face was very near his.

This time something hit him and hard. He was pushed over into Mary, and they fell down onto the grass in one big heap. At the last minute, Blake tucked to the side so he did not collapse directly onto Mary and kept Opal free from collision. He looked up to see Anton's dog right before the animal licked his face.

"Get off me, Patches!" Blake pushed the large collie off of him. "Everyone all right?"

The girls leapt up to pet Patches. Even Opal wrestled out of Blake's arms. Mary shook next to him.

"Mary?" Was she hurt? He rolled to his side to look at her. She was laughing. "You scared me. I thought you were shaking from pain."

"You are right. Your dragon game was better than princesses."

"You practically issued a challenge, you know. Tomorrow you can be a princess, and I promise not to interfere." Blake stood and helped Mary up.

Mary sighed. "You know, I wasn't afraid of you. Opal, on the other hand, makes a furious dragon. I never would have guessed a one-year-old to be so very terrifying."

Blake watched the girls chase after the dog. "Careful, girls. She'll bite if you pull her tail." He turned to find Mary staring at him. "What?"

"I forgot how good you were with children."

"That's because I'm still a child myself. I never grew up."

Mary bit back her smile. "Sounds about right, except I've never seen a child with such broad shoulders."

Blake straightened. "Admiring my physique, are you?"

Mary's smile dropped. "The moment I think you have changed, and you remind me you haven't." She turned to the girls. "Who wants biscuits and jam?"

"I was joking," Blake said, shaking his head. What he would give to know why she was mad at him. He'd been teasing for years about being the best looking in the neighborhood. If he couldn't be rich or titled, he had to claim something. It was a running joke and no more. Sighing, he watched Mary herd the girls back toward the front of the keep, like pretty little maids all in a row.

He dusted the grass off his breeches and went to collect his horse. He was no closer to finding himself a bride today than he was yesterday. He'd even gone to Anton for advice this morning, only to be interrupted by the children. Now, here he was again, heading home to listen to his mother harp on him or hide with his father and his beetle collection.

Turning, he took one last look at Mary's fleeting image. Lud, but she was beautiful. He could easily convince himself to care for her. He did need a wife. He rubbed his chin with his thumb. No, his best friends would kill him. He'd had thoughts like this before, and it was best to suppress them as fast as they came.

It was too late.

Her blue eyes sparkled like sapphires in his mind, and he could feel her warm body pressed close. His breath caught in his chest. He had to physically shake his head to rid himself of her image. It didn't matter how much fun they had together, or the myriad of memories that tied them fast in a permanent connection. Mary deserved to be loved, and Blake didn't know the first thing about the subject.

Not Mary, anyone but Mary.

Chapter Seven

Mary pushed all the blocks in the nursery into a pile. "Let's build another castle."

Gloria shook her blonde little head. "We already built three castles. I'm tired of blocks. Can't we play with Mr. Gunther again?"

Frowning, Mary stole a glance at the door for the millionth time that day. Where was Blake? He'd been absent all yesterday, but two days in a row? He must be ill. That was it. Nothing else would have kept him away. "Why don't I see if I can find him, shall I? You stay here with Hannah, and color your mother another picture."

Mary picked up her skirt and skipped down the stairs in search of Anton or Terrance. They ought to know where Blake was if anyone did. She froze at the bottom when she realized Lord Templeton stood just inside the front door. Heat engulfed her.

"Lady Mary," Lord Templeton said. "I thought you would stumble with the speed you took those stairs."

Mary choked on her sharp inhale and coughed several times in her hands. "I did not know you were here. Forgive me."

"That much is obvious, but do not be embarrassed. I came to call on your family."

"Please," she pointed to the drawing room. She turned to a footman. "Send a maid for my mother and brothers." She took a seat on a chair opposite him. Seeing Lord Templeton again reminded her of their enjoyable conversation from their dinner several nights previously. If only she had met Lord Templeton before Blake. No, that was ridiculous. She'd known Blake since her birth.

"How are you settling into your home? Is your butler still sneezing?"

"No, actually," Lord Templeton said, chuckling. "It turns out it was a small cold. My relief was palpable."

"And your housekeeper? Does she still frighten you?"

"She is terrifying. I—" Lord Templeton was cut off by her mother's entrance.

"We are so glad you have come to call on us, Lord Templeton." Mother gave Mary an overexcited smile, and Mary lowered her brow in annoyance. She wasn't in the mood to entertain guests.

More voices came from the foyer. Her brothers stepped into the doorway, followed by Blake. Mary looked past her brother and speared Blake with a glare. He pretended not to notice, but that only made her angrier.

Her brothers flanked her mother on the sofa, forcing Blake to sit near Mary.

"I heard you acquired a new horse," Terrance said to Lord Templeton, who was seated across the room from her, "with an exceptional bloodline."

"Indeed," Lord Templeton said. "I wanted to start building up my new stables."

"Mother here is adamant that we only house *practical* horses." Anton put his arm around his mother. "But Gunther here has a beauty that is worth looking at."

"Perhaps we should have us a bit of a race," Lord Templeton said.

Mary leaned over in time to see Blake's eyes gleam.

"You must've learned of our racecourse east of here. I must warn you," Blake said. "I'm terribly competitive."

Lord Templeton's smile answered before he did. "So am I."

Anton began drilling him about his horse, but Mary tuned him out. She cleared her throat, getting Blake's attention.

"Where have you been?" she whispered, trying not to move her mouth and alert the others to their secret conversation.

"Down the hall . . ."

Mary's eyes narrowed. "The girls have been expecting you since yesterday. They didn't forget your promise to play with them, and neither did I."

Blake shifted uncomfortably. Good. He should be uncomfortable. She could not rely on him for anything. At least not anymore.

"Your mother . . ." Blake waited until the other conversation picked up again. "Your mother would not like me spending so much time with you."

Mary's brow furrowed, and she eyed her mother. "Why? Did she say something to you?" Blake pretended interest in the other conversation. Without thinking, she hit him in the shoulder. All the eyes in the room turned to her. "Uh, just a fly. Carry on."

Blake's eyes nailed her to her seat. "Just a fly?" He looked anywhere but at her. "You are surprisingly strong," he whispered. He rubbed his arm discreetly the moment the subject of horses was brought up again.

Horses — one of Blake's favorite subjects — and she wasn't giving him a chance to participate. But why was he not telling her about what her mother said? "Blake Gunther. If you don't tell me what my mother said, I am going to tell everyone in this room that you named your first horse True Love and kissed her after every ride."

Blake did not so much as look at her, but his cheeks colored at the memory she'd recreated, and she knew she had won.

"Later," he said through the side of his mouth.

"When?"

His head turned a subtle notch so his eyes were on her. "Wicked girl, pay attention to Lord Templeton before he thinks you are in love with me."

Mary's cheeks flamed for the second time after Lord Templeton witnessed her running down the stairs. She resisted smacking Blake's arm again. No, she would save that for later.

"I heard you received a few guests this last week," Lord Templeton said. "The vicar stopped by and shared the news about your daughter and asked I keep her in my prayers, which I will of course. Is there anything more I can do?"

Mary remembered Blake asking a similar question. But there was no way her mother would let Lord Templeton help with the children. He was practically a stranger.

"Your company is the best distraction you could give us," Mother said. "Would you care to come to dinner tomorrow night? I know the others would be as pleased as I am."

Lord Templeton glanced at Mary and smiled. "If you insist. I tire of dining alone in that great house."

"Oh, yes," Mary said. "You must come." She said it with a touch of too much enthusiasm to make up for the lack of participation in the earlier conversation. Heaven forbid, Lord Templeton think she was uninterested. It would ruin her plan completely.

Lord Templeton made his excuses and said goodbye, with the promise to return the following night.

They all stood to see him off, but Mary turned to Blake before he could disappear. "At least stop in the nursery before you disappear."

Blake turned to Lady Crawford. She gave him a quick nod and a sheepish smile. Blake put out his arm and Mary took it, though she'd rather hit him again. Once they were up the stairs, Blake pulled her arm closer in his and put his hand on hers. For a moment, Mary forgot to breathe. It was just like the other day when they'd played dragons. Blake had no idea what his touch did to her.

"I'm sorry I deserted you. I promise, I had every intention of helping."

"Did you really?" Mary wanted to believe him, but she was skeptical about everything these days.

"Someone saw us on the lawn yesterday. You remember. When we fell down on the grass?"

Mary gasped. "And they told my mother."

"Unfortunately, she was the someone who saw us."

"My mother never thought twice about mishaps like that before my coming out." Mary put her free hand up to rub her temple. "She didn't breathe a word to me about it. Why would she speak to you and not to her own daughter?"

Blake stopped outside the nursery door. "There might be some rumors flying about me around certain circles."

"Go on," Mary encouraged.

"How do I put this?" Blake pulled at his cravat.

Mary reached up and tugged his hand away. "Stop, you'll make a mess of it. Just tell me what everyone is saying about you. I have no doubt heard the rumors anyway. I am not as naive as you think."

Blake stared at her. "What have you heard?"

"That you are an idiot," Mary smiled coyly.

"Very funny. If I am to tell you anything, you must promise to believe what I tell you is the truth."

His gaze unnerved her. She forced herself to focus. "I will be honest with my opinion, as always."

"Ha," he said, looking quite uncomfortable. "I would expect no less from you." He tapped his foot a few times, then finally seemed ready to share. "Some have taken my flirtations and misconstrued them into . . . an act . . . of ungentlemanly proportions."

"One could construe a great many conclusions with such vagueness. Let me guess, my mother is afraid you will now ruin me with your sullied reputation?"

"Lady Crawford trusts me more than I deserve, but she is careful, and her caution does her credit. She is right to want the best for you. I am certainly not the man she would imagine . . . uh, well you know."

Mary wanted nothing more than to know his opinion of such an insinuation, but that would hardly be in her realm of courage. "Don't take it too much to heart. My mother loves you like you are her own son, and she reprimands them too." Then she paused. "Are the rumors true? I will know if you are lying."

"Mary, no. I could never . . . well, you know my nature. I am not completely without morals. How can I help it if all the ladies are in love with me?"

Mary groaned and pulled away from Blake. "Your conceit is predictable."

"If I am as predictable as you say, would you believe me capable of harming another woman?"

Mary thought about last Season and how Blake had broken her heart. "Physical harm, no. However, I have complete assurance you could crush a girl's hopes and dreams."

Blake followed Mary into the nursery. "How could you say that? I am a gentleman. I live by the same code of honor as your brothers."

The children saw him and ran to hug his legs. He picked up Gloria with one arm and Claire with another. "I have missed my little princesses."

"If you missed us, then why did you not come yesterday?" Gloria asked. Her little lips turned down into a pout, very much like her aunt's.

"An evil sorceress forbade me from coming and locked me in a tower with two trolls." Gloria's eyes grew wide. "But a beautiful maiden rescued me from the throngs of despair and carried me all the way to your castle."

"Aunt Mary carried you?" Gloria asked, her nose scrunched in confusion.

Mary shook her head. "He is much too bigheaded for me to carry anywhere." Then she eyed Blake. "What would my mother say if she discovered you had called her a sorceress and thought my brothers trollish?"

Claire kept Blake from responding. "I can't find my castle," she complained.

Blake's grin was lopsided. "Come on, Mary. Find the girls their castle."

"Your castle is under the table." Mary pulled Claire out of Blake's arms and over to the table where Hannah sat knitting. "Sorry Hannah, it looks like we are intruding on your peace."

"I want a castle too," Gloria whined. "There aren't any more tables, and I'm older. Make Claire move."

Blake pulled out two chairs and quickly threw a blanket across the top. "There, problem solved."

Mary sat down gingerly on the ground and situated her dress around her legs. It would be easy to pretend she was married to Blake and these were their children. In moments like this, she could see the good in Blake and understand why her heart could not let go. He looked over just then and gave her a teasing smile. For a moment, she could see worry in the back of his eyes. The self-assured man she knew never really worried. Did he? Was there more to the rumors than he was letting on? Mary believed Blake to be an insufferable flirt, but she also knew there was more depth than he let many see, like his loyalty to her family. Unfortunately, the older they grew, the more distant Blake became with his emotions. He was forever smiling like nothing ever got him down. She didn't believe it for a moment.

Chapter Eight

Blake arrived late to Banbury Castle the next afternoon. He wasn't surprised to find Mary sitting in the garden on a blanket, sketching away with the girls by her side. He took his time walking to greet them, his mind spinning around with other things.

To his mother's delight, he had accompanied her to call on two possible candidates for him to court only hours before. Miss Grover was easy enough to converse with, but he had absolutely no attraction to her. She was poor, and his mother repeated the sentiment over and over, reminding him that such a wife would not be equal company for regular visits with the earl and his family at Banbury. To marry without love, and to give up his friends at the same time, did not exactly motivate him.

The second visit was more promising. Blake had met Miss Cartwright before as a friend of Mary's, but she'd been away at a finishing school for young ladies. Her flawless complexion and easy smile set her up to be a pleasant sort. By her parents' esteem, he reasoned she would no doubt bring money to their marriage and had enough affluence already to circulate with those at Banbury.

"Mr. Gunther!" Gloria said, racing toward him with a small paper in her hand. "Look at my flower. Aunt Mary showed me how to draw one."

Blake took the paper, surprised to see it actually resembled a flower. "Well done, Gloria."

Mary didn't look up as he crossed over to her. She was intent on her sketch. He leaned over, amazed as always to see her drawing so similar to its subject.

"You ought to try drawing your father some time. I should love to see his face again."

"I thought you would sing the Mary Contrary song and ask me how my garden grows."

"I was tempted, but I am already on your bad side."

She suppressed a smile. "Come sit awhile. I will reward you by showing you one of my favorite sketches."

He obeyed and sat on the corner of the blanket, pulling one leg up to support his arm.

Flipping back a few pages in her sketchbook, Mary stopped on an image that made Blake's heart squeeze: a picture of the late earl and his wife dancing. The details were muted unlike the precise lines of her flowers, and the effect made the couple seem almost dream-like.

"He loved to dance with your mother."

Mary sighed, tracing around her father's face so as not to smudge it. "He put up such a fuss about every ball that no one would have believed it unless they saw it with their own eyes."

"I've never seen two people more in love."

Mary turned and her eyes connected with his for the first time that day. "Nor I. Do you think you will ever feel that way about someone?"

Blake blanched. He had not expected such a question. Luckily, Opal took an opportunity to pull Claire's hair at that moment. He rescued Claire, and Mary scooped up Opal. Claire snuggled up against him, pulling a satisfied grin to his mouth. Now the question seemed easy to answer. "I think I could feel the same way your father did when I look at these children. I would do anything for them. Look at how Claire clings to me. She is smitten. I daresay we will be married before twenty years have passed."

Mary rolled her eyes. "She does the same thing when my brothers or I hold her. I gather most three-year-old children find comfort in hugs."

Opal pulled out of Mary's arms to pursue a butterfly. Claire saw it and jumped out of his arms to follow.

"Don't chase it!" Gloria yelled. "I want to draw it." The young girl sighed and dropped her paper to follow her sisters.

Mary picked up her sketchbook again and flipped to a new page.

Blake stretched out his long legs on the blanket, settling comfortably next to Mary again. He looked over to see her outlining a rough shape of a head and shoulders. "Who are you drawing now?"

"Perhaps you could guess in a moment or two."

He watched her work for a minute, impressed by her honed skill. "Have you showed your mother the picture of her and your father dancing?"

"No. You know I don't like to share my sketches with anyone."

"I never understood that." Though she would not share them with others, he appreciated the special privilege of seeing her art.

"There is so much pressure already to be exactly one way. I want one area of my life to be without censure or comparison."

"Your mother could only ever appreciate your talent."

Mary shrugged. "Maybe, but then she would want me to show everyone, and I cannot guarantee that someone else won't have an opinion. Besides, many of my drawings feel sacred. It's like putting a piece of my heart on paper."

No one was more passionate than Mary. Whatever she did, she did it with heart. Including when she decided to hate him.

"Why are you smiling at me like that?"

"I was just wondering what other sketches are in that book. Not even I have seen them all."

"You are lucky I have shown you any of them at all."

"I am the one who taught you to sketch."

"Yes, well, that was ages ago." She bent back over her drawing, shading the face and adding details to the cheekbones.

"Is that . . .?"

"Yes."

"Why would you draw Lord Templeton? Don't tell me he has captured your fancy. I did wonder the last time we saw him."

"And why not?" Mary asked, turning to face him again. She leaned back on one hand and smiled like she knew something he didn't. "Terrance said I made quite the impression on him. Just this morning, he sent flowers."

Gunther's smile wavered, but he pulled it tight. "I don't know why I didn't see it before. You two would make a smashing couple."

She grinned.

Well, that had been his test and she either was an excellent actress or truly was interested in Lord Templeton. The Mary he knew would not just throw herself at a man.

"Where is my portrait?"

Mary blinked and then snorted. Her laugh bubbled out so quickly, it took him off guard.

"What? Is my irresistible charm and good nature too magnanimous for you to encapsulate in a portrait?"

"Oh, I think I could manage." Mary wiped an amused tear from her eye.

"Have you attempted one already?" This he had to know. If Mary gave him one little inkling that she was interested in him, then he would never let Lord Templeton step foot on Banbury grounds again. He might even risk the wrath of her brothers.

What was he saying? Mary had some strange power over him. It was normal for him to forget himself if he stayed too long in her presence. Miss Cartwright was a safer, more predictable choice.

"I have, actually."

Her eyes were teasing him now and he couldn't resist leaning his head closer. "Truly?"

She blushed and nodded. "It wasn't your best side."

His eyebrows rose. "Oh, so this was commissioned in anger."

"I didn't think it fair for you to chase after Miss Bliss when you didn't even know her."

"Ah, the reason for your anger when I arrived home from Rosewood Park."

"Only part of it." Her smile all but disappeared. "Why did you even go? You couldn't possibly have loved her after such a short acquaintance."

Picking at a thread on the blanket, Blake thought how best to answer her. Deep down, he knew that Miss Bliss was another Miss Cartwright. A fleeting fancy. Someone he felt safe to think about but would never really be able to commit to. "My head was turned. Surely you understand that with your recent feelings for Lord Templeton."

Her head dipped down.

"I confess," he continued, "that part of me wanted to protect Anton from getting his heart broken. Looks like I needed to protect him from Terrance, not Miss Bliss."

Mary shrugged. "I thought you cared for someone else before you left."

"Me?" Blake chuckled. "Who did you pin me with? I am a harmless flirt and no more. If I tease a smile from a lonely young woman, the *ton* has me pegged for the father of her children. It's a good thing I am not returning for a London Season until I am married."

A gasp of disbelief emitted from Mary's mouth.

"It's true," Blake said. "I am to be married soon. Aren't you going to congratulate me?"

She leaned back on both hands. "You had me there for a moment."

Blake decided not to press the issue. He was enjoying their easy comradery and bringing up Miss Cartwright would ruin their time together. Sitting next to Mary with the girls entertaining themselves was his idea of a perfect afternoon. Tomorrow, he would remind himself once more that entertaining ideas of Mary was absurd. He didn't need a woman to make him happy, just one to give him back his freedom. Lord Templeton was Mary's equal, not him.

Chapter Nine

"Tomorrow night Lord Templeton will join us for a farewell dinner for Terrance."

Mary sighed. "Yes, Mama."

"What is bothering you?" Lady Crawford asked, looking up from her dressing table. "I thought you found Lord Templeton to be as amiable as I do."

"There is nothing wrong with Lord Templeton. He is perfect," Mary reasoned in an attempt to convince herself. As much as she tried, she could not push her recent time with Blake to the back of her mind. And now Terrance—her greatest ally—was abandoning her. "I am simply thinking of how hard it will be to have Terrance leave." She couldn't bear two such sad conclusions in her mind at the same time.

"I confess, I do not like to think of your brother so far from us."

"Then why does he have to go?" Mary hated thinking of everything changing again. They were just finding their new normal after father's death. "Why can't we continue just as we are?"

"It's the natural way of life for a man and woman to leave their parents and start a new life together. It will be your turn soon enough."

"I don't want to marry if it means saying goodbye to you and my brothers and moving far away."

"I dread the idea of you leaving us too, but when you fall in love, you will see that it's a small sacrifice to make in order to form a new family." Her mother stared at Mary for a moment. Then she turned to her maid. "That will be all, Rachel." When Rachel closed the door, her mother stood and pulled Mary to a pair of chairs by her window. "There is something I have been meaning to speak to you about."

"If it's about the other day on the lawn with Blake, I promise, it was a complete accident."

"It *is* about Mr. Gunther. When Lord Templeton comes tomorrow, you must not let him think your attention is divided. Mr. Gunther is a dear family friend, and he is harmless enough, but you know as well as I that he isn't in any hurry to marry."

"What does that have to do with Lord Templeton?" Mary felt defensive.

"If you were to marry Lord Templeton, you could not have such an easy comradery with Mr. Gunther. It is time to put your childhood friendship aside and focus on the one relationship that matters — the one with your future husband. When Mr. Gunther comes today, I am going to ask if he would no longer visit the nursery."

"But why? The children adore him and he them. I cannot see how this would be good for anyone."

"It's not because of them, but because of you."

Mary folded her arms and turned to look through the window. The view of the orchard only reminded her of Blake's silly request for a romantic stroll. Her mother was right. The time she spent with Blake only made her heart more vulnerable. All morning she had been filled with hope, but it only ever set her up for more disappointment. "All right."

Her mother sighed, reaching for her gloves and slipping them over her hands. "It will be one more change we will have to accustom ourselves to, but Mr. Gunther will understand."

"I've invited Miss Cartwright for dinner at the end of the week," Mrs. Gunther said over breakfast.

Blake scooped up his coddled eggs. "I will be there."

His mother's lips pulled back into a pleased expression—a look rarely directed his way. His sisters were in the other room with his father, and he could hear their gushing sighs over their new shawls from India. The real prize was a special beetle specimen shipped all the way from Bombay. And what did Blake get? More matchmaking.

"I thought Miss Cartwright so genteel. Not overexcited like so many new girls out in society but not overly demure either."

"A great example for my sisters, then," he teased. He had better not let his mother know he was even remotely open to pursuing Miss Cartwright. His mother would have their wedding invitations copied on the finest paper by nightfall.

"Your sisters are not invited to dine with us."

"Why not?"

"They talk too much. I thought about inviting another couple, but I daresay it would divide conversation. I want you and Miss Cartwright to have as much opportunity to speak as possible."

"Does she know about the rumors?"

"Everyone has heard the rumors. You are fortunate they are willing to overlook such things. Your connections to the earl are your saving grace."

Suddenly, his stomach soured, and he could not finish his breakfast. "Speaking of his lordship, he has need of me at Banbury," he lied, wiping his lips with his napkin. "I should go straight away."

Of all his faults, dishonesty was not one of them. False flattery . . . on occasion. Stretching the truth . . . when necessary. But this was an outright lie. The pressure was getting to him. He bid his mother goodbye and found his horse in the stable as ready for a ride as Blake was.

The steady cadence of the horse did little to settle his stomach, but the fresh air and peace were worth the short trip. A castle groomsman took his horse when he arrived, allowing Blake to enter the keep without detouring to the stables. He hoped at least someone was up and about inside. He would dearly like to talk about anything other than shawls, beetles, or wives.

Pearl let him inside, and he handed off his hat.

"Mr. Gunther," Lady Crawford called from the corridor just outside Anton's study. "Might you join us for a moment?"

"Gladly, my lady." Blake wondered what they would need his opinion for. The last time they'd spoken privately, it had been to reprimand him. He hoped it wasn't that. A faint scent of leather and musty books greeted him as he stepped into the room. Blake took in the serious faces of both mother and son. "It isn't Jillian, is it?"

"I haven't had word for days," Lady Crawford said. "If I haven't received news to reassure me by the end of the week, I will go to her myself." She motioned for him to sit. Once he did, they sat too.

The study was a narrow rectangle and perfect for one or two people, but three felt nearly claustrophobic to him. He ached to open the only window behind him. "If not Jillian, what has you both so solemn?"

"You," Anton said, not mincing words.

"Me?" Blake sat back and folded his arms across his chest. "Oh, come on. Not you, too. I promise, I haven't seduced a woman all week."

"Mr. Gunther!" Lady Crawford put her hand over her heart.

He bit the inside of his cheek. Patience wasn't exactly his forte this morning. "I apologize. Most of the neighborhood has condemned me, and I thought at least this family would find the rumors a touch ridiculous."

Lady Crawford put her hand on his arm. "Blake dear," she said, dropping pretenses. "It's not the rumors but about Mary again."

He braced himself. "What is worrying you?" If it was Lord Templeton, Blake would have no problem recalling some of his college boxing moves.

Anton cleared his throat. "Mother and I are hopeful she and Lord Templeton will make a match. It would be easier if you were not in the picture. I told Mother you would understand."

"I am not sure I do."

Lady Crawford squeezed his arm gently. "You and Mary are good friends, but it's hard for a suitor to understand the nature of your relationship. While we all know the two of you are like brother and sister and would never suit as a couple, Lord Templeton might think you are the target of Mary's attention, not him."

No matter how he had trained himself to lighten moods such as this, he could not pull his lips into a smile. The phrase *like brother and sister and would never suit* repeated itself in his mind. "I see. Would you like me to bow out of Terrance's goodbye dinner tonight?"

"No," Lady Crawford said quickly. "Terrance would see that as a slight to him."

Blake cleared his throat. "I will do my best not to speak to Mary tonight then."

"There's more," Anton said.

Blake wasn't sure if he could handle anymore, especially coming from his best friend. "Well? Out with it."

"Mother and I think it best for you to stay at your place for the next few weeks. It's not like you aren't welcome here at Banbury — we consider you family — it's simply that . . ."

"You must maintain appearances," Blake finished.

Lady Crawford sighed. "This isn't coming out as I wished it to."

"Please," Blake said holding up his hand to silence her grievances. "Do not worry yourself on my account. I am sure there are dark summers in everyone's lives, and this just happens to be mine." He laughed at his poor joke, but it just made the others look miserable. "I was jesting. Of course, I want Mary to be happy as much as either of you do. If Mary and Lord Templeton are hoping to court, then I will gladly give them room to do so."

"See, Mother," Anton said. "I told you Gunther would understand. There isn't a better chap in all the world." Then Anton's eyes connected with Blake's. "Looks like I will have to come visit you at your place for a change, hmm? Although your father might ask about my beetle collection he started for me. I will have to admit I burned it to avoid nightmares of bugs crawling all over me."

"You two keep discussing the details," Lady Crawford said, standing. "I want to check on the menu for tonight with cook again." She put her hand on Blake's shoulder and rubbed it affectionately. "We'll miss you even though you're just a few miles away."

"Thank you, Lady Crawford." He knew she loved him, but clearly not as much as her own children like he'd once thought.

"I'll see myself out," he said to Anton once the door shut behind Lady Crawford.

Anton's face softened, and his brows creased with concern. "Make a quick goodbye to the children, will you? The older two keep asking after you, and it wouldn't be right to keep them wondering."

"Are you sure your mother would approve?"

Anton flicked the feather on his quill. "I'll try to head her off so you can have a moment."

"Just like old times when we were planning pranks, eh?"

Anton chuckled. "Except this time, you aren't going to do anything foolish."

Blake stood and walked to the door. "I might kidnap Opal. She likes me better than the rest of you."

"Not if you want to get on my mother's good side again."

"I'm beginning to wonder if I ever was." Blake's joke held shreds of truth. Perhaps his own mother was right, and she was never right. It was time for Blake to move on like the rest of the world.

Chapter Ten

Mary had seen Blake ride up to the castle from her view in the small alcove. Then she'd waited, just tucked behind the top of the stairs, and stole a glimpse of her mother cornering him. It did not take much deducing to discover that the subject of their conversation was her. Once her mother had an idea, she stuck to it.

Tears dripped from her eyes as she waited. Her plan for Terrance to find her a suitor had worked in all the wrong ways. Now Mary was doomed to have Lord Templeton as her fate. The door opened twice before Blake exited. Her breath caught, and she slipped back into her alcove. She did not want him to see her cry.

His steps grew louder as he finished climbing the stairs and drew closer to her. A hiccup escaped and she slammed her hand over her mouth.

His steps ceased right in front of her hiding spot.

It was her curse. More often than not, she developed hiccups when she cried. She held her breath and didn't so much as flinch until the footsteps started up again. Blake was no doubt on his way to the nursery.

When Mary was sure the corridor was clear, she snuck out of her hiding place and hurried to find Terrance. She pushed open his door, startling him.

Terrance's surprised expression turned into feigned annoyance. "I could have been dressing, you know."

"I knew you were packing." She took several heavy steps to his bed and sat down. "I've made a mess of everything."

"Gunther again?"

"Yes," Mary said, not even caring how whiney her voice sounded. "What advice do you have for me?"

"Do whatever you can to secure Lord Templeton's affections at dinner tonight."

"And that will make Blake wildly jealous?" Mary wasn't sure it would work.

"No," Terrance said, tossing a stack of handkerchiefs into his trunk. "My advice is literal. It's high time you consider options outside of Blake Gunther."

His pronouncement depressed her further. "All right. I'll really try this time."

"Good, because my patience with my friend is wearing thin, and if he makes you cry one more time, he'll live to regret it."

Mary's lips quivered, but she managed a watery smile for her brother. "He won't, because I am going to take your advice. But if Blake gets under my skin again, I will let you do your worst. Go for his nose, will you? His face is far too perfect for his own good."

Terrance chuckled. "I'm going to miss you, Mary Contrary."

Mary's smile flipped into a scowl. "Terrance Hadley!"

He put his hands up to beg for mercy. "I swear I said your nickname with only the utmost affection."

She rolled her eyes and stood to leave. "Perhaps I ought to write to Miss Bliss and tell her just how charming you really are." She stuck her tongue out at her brother and left his room with her threat hanging over him. A small smile crept back over her lips. Terrance was lucky to have found someone. Tonight would be her turn.

Chapter Eleven

Blake kissed and hugged the children but found he was disappointed Mary was not with them. An emptiness settled over him that he could not explain. It stayed with him all day until he returned to Banbury Castle that night for Terrance's farewell dinner.

The ache in his heart lifted the exact moment he saw Mary. She was laughing, and her joy bubbled over and warmed him. He moved closer, only to freeze when he saw who she was laughing with—Lord Templeton.

The rest of the night was filled with flirtatious banter between Mary and Lord Templeton, and Blake found it quite appalling. When dinner and port were over, they gathered back in the drawing room to visit.

"How is it possible we share the same favorite foods? What else do I need to know about you?" Mary turned her head to the side and admired Lord Templeton openly. "You must have a disagreeable aunt or I will be determined to think you perfect."

Blake closed his eyes for a moment and pictured Mary and his new enemy exchanging vows at the altar. The image was like a punch to Blake's gut. He marched over to Terrance, standing by the fireplace. "Are you as disgusted as I am by this revolting scene?"

"What? Mary?"

Blake glanced back to see Mary lean forward and flutter her eyelashes. He could vomit on the man's perfectly shined Hessian boots. "Have you ever seen her throw herself at a man like she is now?"

"It's harmless flirtations. Nothing at all to someone like you, Romeo."

Blake wondered at the hard glint in Terrance's eyes. "Not you too." Terrance stood up straight, reminding Blake how much shorter he was than his friend.

"When is the birth of your child anyhow?"

Blake's anger erupted at the words. He fisted his hand and drew back to sock Terrance.

Someone caught his hand from behind. Anton.

"Contain yourself," Anton warned. "You knock Terrance's teeth out, and my mother will have you banned from Mary's presence for the rest of eternity."

Blake growled and took several short breaths.

"Simmer, good man," Terrance said, stepping back. "If it's just a rumor, then you have no reason to be so sour."

"Is that what you think? That it's a simple rumor without a shred of truth?" Blake asked, crossing his arms to keep from killing someone. "Because I want to know who my true friends are."

Terrance didn't answer. Instead, he swung his eyes to Mary.

Blake turned to Anton. "Tell me."

Anton put his hand on his waist. "You tell us."

"All right," Blake said, ready to confess despite his injured pride. "There is no way under heaven that I am anyone's father."

Terrance sighed, still keeping his eyes on his sister. "It's one thing to believe you when it's just us. It's another when our sister's honor is at stake."

"And why would it be?" Blake asked louder than he should have. The others shushed him. He just didn't understand what was going on here.

"We aren't fools," Anton said. "We have eyes. And the sparks flying between you and Mary are worse than any lightning storm I've ever seen."

"Then what is happening right now?" Blake asked, pointing to Mary practically throwing herself at the gentleman. If he didn't know her better, he'd think she was a brazen hussy.

Terrance answered rather simply. "Mary is either trying to forget you or to drive you to your knees." He finally looked at Blake. "I'd say it's working."

"She's driving me mad." Blake rubbed the back of his neck. Agitation seized his muscles, causing him to tense everywhere.

"That's love for you." Terrance gave Blake a coy smile.

His calm demeanor and dry humor did nothing but annoy Blake. "Mary is like a sister to me."

Anton's laugh joined Terrance's. He looked at Mary, who glared at them. Blake put his back to her again.

"Fine. So, I care for Mary. Is it such a crime? Am I to be drawn and quartered by my best friends?"

Anton slapped Blake on the back. "It's about time you admitted it. Does she know?"

Blake sniffed back his angry emotions. "Maybe."

Terrance grinned. "That's coward for no."

"I'm leaving. Tell your bewitching sister goodnight for me." Blake didn't hide the contempt from his voice.

"Tell her yourself," Terrance said, with a flourish of his arm in Mary's direction.

Blake made a cutting glare at the turncoat and forced himself to face his misery. He stalked over to the others.

"If you will pardon my interruption," Blake said in the sweetest voice he could procure under such maddening circumstances, "but I would like to thank Lady Crawford for the delicious meal and bid you all goodnight."

"Leaving so soon?" Mary said, without any real care in her voice.

"I am overtired, Lady Mary. But I am sure your present company will keep you perfectly entertained in my absence."

Mary looked almost guilty for a moment, but she recovered quickly. She gave him a placating smile. "Yes, you'd better hurry home and rest. Goodnight."

Lady Crawford and the gentlemen murmured their parting words and Blake forced himself from Mary's presence for self-preservation. What was he going to do? Even his friends believed him capable of such indiscretions. Perhaps he'd gone too far in his flirtations this last Season. He'd been a fool.

How could he possibly earn Mary's trust again? And before it was too late. He was already banned from the house.

Instead of stalking from the room, he returned to his friends. "You've got to help me."

"What exactly are your intentions?" Terrance asked. "Because if it isn't marriage, then you can count me out."

Blake turned to Anton, who was nodding his agreement.

"I just decided two minutes ago that I was interested in her. Can't I have a little time to think?"

Anton gestured to the others. "Take all the time you need, but we can't guarantee our sister will still be available."

"Does that mean you will help me scare Templeton away?"

"Define *help*," Terrance said. "I leave in the morning."

"Don't look at me," Anton said. "Templeton is a swell man, and I need his advice on land management. He's better informed than my steward."

Blake sighed. "Very well. I will simply be a one-man army. I will convince Mary that I am the better choice, and I will do it all while avoiding her and Banbury for your mother's sake."

"Sounds simple."

Blake nodded. "I like to keep things as uncomplicated as possible. Goodnight friends. Put in a good word for me once you are completely convinced I'm not a rake."

When Blake finally mounted his horse, he pushed his hat down and spurred his animal into a hard run. Try as he might, Blake would never be happy again as a bachelor. It didn't matter how impossible his situation had become. His mother's long-awaited moment had happened; Blake Gunther was in love.

Chapter Twelve

Mary expected to say goodbye to Terrance, but she was not ready to say goodbye to her mother too. It had been three days since she'd seen Blake, and Mary needed her mother.

"Can't we all go with you?" Mary asked. "The girls would love to see their mother as much as I would my sister."

"Jillian needs quiet and rest," her mother said. "I realize now that I should not have left you alone during my last trip. Thankfully, Anton will be here for you if you need anything at all."

Mary threw her arms around her mother and squeezed her tightly. "I shall miss you."

"I'll miss you too. Take care of the children."

"Of course."

After waving goodbye, Mary made her way to the nursery. Only Opal and Claire were playing with their nurse.

"Where is Gloria?" Mary asked.

"She said she was tired and went and put herself in her bed."

The children's sleeping quarters were next door to their playroom. "I hope she is not getting sick," Mary said. She sat down and played a few games with the younger two, passing the morning away.

When a tea tray came in with a platter of food for the children, Mary stood and arched her back to release the tension from sitting on the floor. "I will check on Gloria to see if she is feeling well enough to eat."

When she opened the door to the children's bed chamber, she did not see Gloria. Each little bed was empty. Mary walked into the room and searched every corner to make sure she was not hiding or had not fallen asleep somewhere she shouldn't.

"Gloria?" Mary called a few times. She hurried back to the nursery. "Gloria is not in her room."

Hannah's face puckered in confusion, deepening the wrinkles around her mouth. "Where could she have gone to? I will check outside, and you alert the servants to search the house. Don't worry yet. Children have a way of wandering off and are generally closer than you think."

"You are likely right," Mary said. She could hear a faint echo from that morning when she reassured her mother that she would take care of the children. Mary would do anything to prevent harm from coming to any of the girls. "I'll ask the other servants."

An hour later, Mary's hands clenched and her breathing quickened in pure panic mode. She met Anton in front of the main door. "Any luck?"

"The stable is clear, and I still have servants searching the grounds."

"Oh, Anton. Jillian will kill me. Wait. This will kill her."

"Stop it, Mary," Anton said, putting his hand on her arm. "We'll find her. We used to run and hide as children. Ask Hannah if they quarreled at all. I bet Gloria was upset by something."

"I'll ask right away." She spun and ran back up the stairs to the nursery. When she made it there, she found Hannah bouncing Opal on her hip.

"Any luck?"

"No, but could you tell me what you remember about this morning? What sort of mood was Gloria in before she put herself to sleep?"

"She'd been particularly sulky, your ladyship."

"Was there a reason why?"

"I thought she might be missing her parents, what with Lady Crawford leaving and all. Gloria did ask after Mr. Gunther, but I said I didn't know when we would see him again."

"Did this upset her further?"

"Yes, she was sad, but she often gets that way when overtired."

Mary sighed. "Did she say anything more about Mr. Gunther?"

"No. I explained he lived just over the bridge and, if she was lucky, she might see him this afternoon. Mr. Gunther is never absent from Banbury for any long period of time."

"Just over Banbury Bridge . . ." Mary thought out loud. "I remember telling Gloria where the bridge was. You don't suppose she tried to walk to Mr. Gunther's house, do you?"

Hannah pulled Opal closer. "Gloria can be quite headstrong when she gets an idea."

"Then I must send someone to search along the road." Mary hiked up her gloves. "Thank you for your help." She rushed back downstairs.

Anton was pacing in the foyer. "Any ideas?"

"Yes, Gloria might have tried to make it to Blake's."

"Over the Oxford Canal?"

"Yes. I'll fetch my bonnet. You ride along the road in the direction of Grimsbury, and I will take the shortcut. Let's see if we can find her."

"I'll have two horses saddled." The tail of his coat flipped up as he whirled toward the door.

"Help us, please," Mary prayed.

Blake did not sleep well, and a headache gnawed at the base of his head. Thoughts of how to rebrand his person flitted through his mind. He'd always been a confident man, but now self-doubt seemed to paralyze him. What if Mary didn't want him? What if her heart already belonged to Lord Templeton?

"Don't pace in here," his mother said, from her nearly permanent seat in the drawing room. "If you think to change my mind with this childlike display, you are disillusioned."

"Oh, pardon me, Mother. I must be sleepwalking. I had no idea I'd even come in here."

"Why don't you take that beast of yours out for a ride? It's too humid for my taste, but you don't ever seem to care."

"Maybe I will," Blake said. He'd have to stay away from Banbury, but it didn't mean there weren't other places to ride to.

"Once I put my foot down, I will not alter my direction," his mother muttered as Blake walked out.

A stable boy brought his horse out to him, saddled and ready to ride, before Blake could register the passage of time. He really was in his head today. Never had Blake been so strapped for solutions before. He didn't know the first thing about love, and marriage frightened him worse than any nightmare. There were so many risks . . . losing Mary and being forever unhappy or winning Mary and then dragging her down with him.

"Blake!"

Blake looked up to see Mary riding towards him. It wasn't even a daydream. As she came nearer, he could see the lines of concern around her face. "What is it?"

"Gloria is missing. We've searched the house and grounds and can't find her anywhere. Please tell me you've seen her."

"Here? No, I haven't."

Mary's eyes closed briefly, and he could sense the overwhelming worry building inside her. "I don't know where to look. Hannah mentioned to Gloria where you lived, so I had hoped I would find her here."

"There are a good three miles between my house and yours, and Gloria is on foot. She could be anywhere." Blake pulled himself up onto his horse and turned his head to search the landscape. "Where have you looked already?"

Mary filled him in, and then pointed to the road. "Let's search this end of the road and meet up with Anton. Perhaps he has already found her." Her eyes darted across the garden to the tree line and then back to the road.

"Mary," Blake said, "we will find her."

She met his gaze, and her tight posture seemed to relax. "Yes, of course."

There was still several hours of daylight left, which was on their side, but there was also the canal to worry about. Blake nudged his horse, and they started a slow trot down the road. Mary's hands were tight on her reins, putting her horse a little on edge. Blake knew he was going to have to keep her talking while they searched, or her worries would build into hysteria.

"Did Terrance and your mother leave already?"

Mary nodded. "They were both gone by first light."

"How was last night then?"

"Fine."

Blake really didn't want to talk about her previous evening, and he regretted bringing it up. He changed tactics and started calling for Gloria. "Gloria!" he yelled. "Gloria, let's have some sweets together! Come out, wherever you are!"

"That's brilliant," Mary said. She began yelling too and promising treats and parties. Her horse did not take well to the noise and threw his head back in irritation.

"Let's walk, Mary. You're either going to hurt yourself or your horse."

Mary's frown deepened. "You're probably right."

Blake dismounted and then helped Mary to do the same. He gathered both the reins to lead the horses as they walked.

"How do you lose a child?" Mary muttered.

"Very easily," Blake said. "Your brothers and I managed to sneak off more than we were home."

"Yes, but Gloria is alone. What kind of mother will I make if I cannot keep an eye on a child for a single week?"

He was worried too, but he didn't want Mary to know it. "Your concern shows how much you care, which is an excellent estimation of what sort of mother you will be. I, for one, think I will make an excellent father." Blake fluffed his hair and did his best prideful face to tease Mary into a smile.

Mary was in no mood to jest. "You want children? You are not ready for such responsibility. You would have to marry first, heaven forbid."

"I want to be married. I told you as much the other day."

"You weren't being serious then, nor are you now. You can't fudge this."

"It's a new idea for me, but I'm being perfectly serious."

They stopped for a moment, and Mary peeked around a clump of overgrown juniper bushes. Then she turned back to him. "Didn't you say the matrons are all against you? Who would you find to marry you?"

Blake wasn't the overly cautious sort, so perhaps he would put it bluntly. Or was it just his intense desire to let Mary know how he felt? "Couldn't *you* marry me?"

Mary didn't even pause in her step. "Me? Don't be ridiculous. We both know this is a silly attempt to keep me from losing my mind with worry."

"Mary, stop!" Blake's words came out more forceful than he intended. His usual smile slipped from his lips along with his easy confidence. "I like you. I like being with you and the kids. This is how I want to spend my days. I am content and have purpose all at once. Don't you understand? I'm happy when I am with you."

"We've been playing pretend, Blake. You'll tire of it soon enough. I know you."

"You knew the old me, Mary. The young, foolish me. But people change." How could he explain what he himself didn't understand? There were new emotions and ideas stealing over his usual rationale. He didn't just want Mary, he needed her.

"Do people change?" She studied him and then looked away. "I've enjoyed our time together. I've needed your help, and you've been there for me. But we'll go to London for the Season and a pretty face will turn your head. Then what? Where will that leave me?"

"Do you really think me so shallow . . . so faithless?"

Mary speared him with a glare. "Do you remember the Duke of Hartley's ball?"

"The ball at the end of last Season — the one before I left to Miss Bliss's house party?"

"I presume you don't remember how many times you danced with me."

He squinted his eyes for a moment and then shrugged.

"You asked me to dance with you three times. But when you asked the third time, my mother intervened and said no."

"I remember now." But Blake didn't understand what she was getting at. "I love to dance with you. We always have a good time when we are together."

"Yes, but what does it mean when you ask a girl to dance with you more than twice at a ball?"

Blake finally comprehended her meaning. "Usually such a privilege is taken when engaged to be married."

"Precisely. Your mannerisms and attentions for weeks made me think you actually cared for me. The next morning after the ball, I heard all about the competition to win Miss Bliss's hand. I pegged you as lighthearted until *this* happened. Then, I realized you had trifled with my affections and others without a second thought. There are dozens of men just like you, but I am holding out for someone with more depth."

Blake cringed, regret turning his stomach. What a fool he had been. "You are right. That was utterly senseless of me. I only let myself think of you as a sister. I've always thought you the prettiest of my acquaintance, but I had never let myself imagine or hope for more."

"You will forget this whole conversation when we return to London." Mary turned away and started yelling for Gloria again. "Where is that girl?"

Blake searched the trees with his eyes, but he couldn't let their conversation end like this. "No need to go to London. We can stay here. Or . . . go anywhere else you want to."

"I'm too upset right now to think clearly. You're confusing me."

"Mary, I swear to you, I will be a loyal husband. These rumors, they are only that. I admit, I've kissed a few girls for sport, but no more. I've never *loved* anyone before. Never knew it was in me to even feel this way. I have never wanted what my parents have, that is for sure. But being with you could never be that way. It would be like this."

Mary laughed lightly. "Us arguing and searching for a lost child. Not exactly an ideal scenario."

"No, us worrying and working together. We'll hash out all our problems and make things work." He knew she was listening, so he pressed on. "I promise, I'm a changed man. I want a family now, where before the thought scared me to death. And . . . you. I want you."

She looked at him now, like she actually might believe he was in earnest. A sort of bewilderment crossed her face. She finally stopped walking again. "I don't know what to say."

Hope leaped inside of him. He could see her eyes softening. This was his chance. "Say you love me too."

Something in her expression darkened. "Everyone knows I've loved you since we were children."

"Impossible. If everyone knew, then I would know."

"Don't tease me." Her tone clipped her words.

She was serious. Mary loved him? Had always loved him? Sure there had been a big brother type worship from her, but not real love. "You're telling me you've loved me all this time?" His breath grew short, and he couldn't hold back a triumphant grin. Not Lord Templeton . . . but him!

Mary turned and started walking again. "Don't let it go to your head."

Blake hurried to her and grabbed her hand. Energy surged from their connection. They both stared at their hands enclosed for a long moment. He stroked his thumb against the back of her glove, his heart pounding. "Too late. My head is so inflated with joy I could fly." He took in her green eyes, brewing with emotion. "Now that I know you love me, nothing can keep us apart!"

She gave him a sad smile. "Blake, you haven't been listening. How can I possibly know if you really love me? I can't start a family with someone who is as passionate as you are about life. You'll tire of me and move on to something new and exciting."

"No one is more passionate than you, Mary darling." He liked being able to call her that. "Come now, what are you saying?"

Mary sputtered, "You could flirt with a broomstick."

"So we won't keep house with any brooms. Easy fix."

Mary covered her face with her free hand.

He had to release his hold on her to unveil her eyes. "Let me prove myself to you. Will you let me kiss you?" She loved him. She really loved him. The powers of heaven seemed to pull him toward her. One kiss, and he was sure to convince her.

She stepped backward. "No! You will have to earn such a privilege."

Blake felt his cheeks heat. He never blushed, but he felt the shame of his past catch up with him. He had been too eager to turn girls' heads in the past. He'd used them to satisfy this emptiness inside of him. He would never take advantage of Mary, though—not intentionally—not ever again.

"I will," Blake said softly. "And I will be patient until you feel you can trust me."

"Help me find Gloria for starters."

"Yes, of course." His timing was terrible. Could he do nothing right? He was supposed to have a knack for all things romantic. Now he felt like he didn't even know how to speak to a woman.

He started calling for Gloria again. This little girl did mean the world to him, even if Mary couldn't see it.

Ahead of them, Blake saw two horses with riders coming up the road.

"It's Anton," Blake said.

"And Lord Templeton. Look! They have Gloria!" Mary picked up her skirts and started running toward them.

Blake squinted, and sure enough, he caught a flash of yellow hair. Relief surged through him. He didn't even care that Lord Templeton was part of the search team. Mary met up with the other two, and Blake walked steadily toward them, allowing Mary to have time to smother Gloria with hugs and kisses.

When he got to them, Blake stuck out his arms, and Gloria leaped into them. She buried her head against him and started crying. "I just wanted to play dragons and princesses. I didn't mean to get lost!"

He rubbed her back and held her tight. "Didn't you hear us?" Blake whispered into her ear. "There is a princess party at the castle right now with tea and cakes. But you have to dress your best and promise to never run away again."

Gloria pulled back. "Right now? I'm missing the party?"

"No, it won't start until you get back."

"But you'll be there, won't you? I want you to be the prince."

Blake looked over at Mary and then back to Gloria. "Not this time, dear. But next time you need me, have nurse Hannah write me a letter, and I promise to write back."

Gloria's mouth formed into a pout. "But I walked all this way."

Anton cleared his throat. "I'll come, Gloria. I can be the prince."

Gloria scrunched her little nose. "You don't know how to play the game."

Blake didn't want to prolong his goodbye. He scooped Gloria up and handed her to Anton. "Your uncle is the closest to a prince I know. But if you ask nicely, I bet he will make an even better donkey and let you ride on his back." Gloria looked up at Anton's generally serious face and giggled.

Blake turned and nodded to Lord Templeton and then gave Mary a quick smile. "Good day, everyone."

"Won't you help me mount?" Mary asked, pointing to her horse.

Blake's lips twitched. "It would be an honor."

They moved behind the horse, which nearly blocked the others' view of them. Then he put his hands on her waist.

"Thank you," she said. She stepped up on her tiptoes and kissed him on the cheek. His insides melted a little at the innocent gesture.

He cleared his throat and lifted her up onto her saddle.

"Goodbye."

Why did that one little word steal away his joy? Did she mean *goodbye* or just an extension of thank you, and I'll see you around?

He watched them ride off, and he wiped his hands down his face. He knew how to capture a lady's attention, but he realized he was absolutely clueless how to win a lady's heart.

Chapter Thirteen

Flowers and several copied poetry verses arrived throughout the next week. Mary smiled and shook her head. Blake certainly was trying. She'd never been on the receiving end of so much attention. She used her thumb to break the seal of yet another letter. Daylight filtered through the drawing room window across the page, illuminating a lovely sketch of two hands clasped together. One was clearly a man's hand by the size of it, and he was clasping a more petite, feminine hand. She knew instantly that it was Blake holding her hand. She remembered how her heart had leapt when Blake had cradled her hand as he expressed his love for her. The gesture made time feel as if it had stopped.

Her whole body warmed at the memory. Could her touch have affected him too? She sighed happily. A knock on the front door sounded from outside the quiet drawing room, interrupting her reverie. Pearl stood in the threshold of the room only a few moments later.

"Mrs. Gunther is here to see you, milady."

Mary folded the letter and tucked it in her sleeve. She stood as Mrs. Gunther hurried into the room and sat down with a heavy thump. "I must know the absolute truth. Are you or are you not scheming with my son for money?"

"Money?" Mary almost laughed, but she bit the insides of her cheek. Mrs. Gunther could be over-the-top on occasion. She stepped closer to her guest. "Mrs. Gunther, really. You know I have no need for money."

"My son has great need for money, and I fear he is using you."

"Why would he need money?"

Mrs. Gunther appraised her for a moment and then lifted her chin. "If you are not privy to our arrangement, and it appears like you are not, then I must be the one to tell you the truth. My son has abused you greatly."

"Mrs. Gunther, I beg you to be frank. I'm completely baffled by what you could mean."

"At the end of the house party at Rosewood, I told Blake he had to remain at home without any of his usual funds until he settled down and married."

Mary's mouth dropped. She blinked several times and then blurted, "You're joking."

"I do not regret being firm with him, only that he thought he should drag your name down with him. It does not sit well with me that he thinks to court you. Not for one minute."

Mary collapsed into the closest chair and without the usual decorum. "You mean . . . he just . . . I can't even fathom."

Mrs. Gunther nodded. "Exactly. My son is useless to me. I wish I could send him to New South Wales with the criminals."

"You were right to tell me, Mrs. Gunther. I must beg your leave. I feel a horrid headache coming on. Forgive me." She stood and stumbled from the room. She made her way to her bedroom and crawled into her bed. When she opened her eyes it was to the silly face she'd drawn of Blake weeks before. Her eyes narrowed in on his bulbous nose. *That idiot. That wretched, wretched man!*

She was going to kill him.

Blake survived dinner with Miss Cartwright without so much as smiling at her. Mary would have been very proud. His mother, on the other hand, had been livid. That is, until he'd explained he was courting Mary — or trying to. His mother's shock had sent her into silence for a whole thirty seconds. Since then, she'd sent him curious looks but not pushed any idea of another girl his way.

Still, it had been a long, arduous week for Blake. Being cooped up was not his forte. He spent all morning crafting an original poem for Mary. He read through the final product and burned it. No use scaring her back to Lord Templeton. Instead, he copied another verse from the professionals and sent it over to the castle.

After visiting with his sisters and enduring their high-pitched stories, he went in search of his father. They had been spending more time together out of necessity, and Blake thought he would give beetle hunting one more try. He hoped his efforts with Mary would pay off soon, or Blake might not be sane long enough to know. He found his father outside, placing a beetle specimen in a clear glass.

"Father, there you are. Would you like me to help you search for beetles or carry your things to the study?"

His father blinked a few times in confusion. "You hate beetles."

"But you love them, and since I want to spend time with you, I thought this might be the best way to do it."

His father bent back to his work. "Fine, I'll tell you. Your mother went in a huff to speak with Lady Crawford."

"What?" This was the last thing Blake expected to hear. "Lady Crawford is still at her daughter's house nursing her back to health." He stood there a moment waiting for his father to comment, but he didn't. "Well, why was Mother in a huff? And why did she need to speak with the countess?"

His father frowned. "I can't remember. I wasn't paying attention." He peered into the transparent cup at his latest find. "Something about you wanting money at any cost."

The blood drained from Blake's face. "Was she going to tell Mary about the bargain?"

His father looked at him through the glass, magnifying his one open eye. "Do you see how the light makes the wings bluer? Fascinating."

Blake clenched his hands at his side. "Yes, I can see that. Very fascinating. Uh, look. I am afraid we will have to do this another time. I can't afford to lose Mary to Mother's grasp."

"Because of the money?" His father set aside the glass and was staring at him. Really staring at him.

"No, I love her. She's the only girl in the world for me."

His father smiled. "Then you'd better hurry."

This counted as a heart-to-heart in Blake's book. He squeezed his father's shoulder affectionately. "Thank you."

He took off at a run toward the stables, calculating how long it would take to have his horse saddled and to ride over. When had his mother left? More importantly, how much damage had she done?

Blake arrived as soon as he could to Banbury Castle. His mother's carriage was pulling out, and he'd been too late. He rode directly up to the front of the house and dismounted, abandoning his prize horse without bothering to tie him up.

Pearl let Blake in a moment later, and Blake hurried to the drawing room. Empty. He turned and took the stairs two at a time. He checked the alcove first — the one he wasn't supposed to know about — since it was on the way to Mary's room. Empty.

He rushed down the corridor to Mary's closed door. He beat on it. "Mary! Mary, open up this instant." He jiggled the door, but it was locked. "Please, love. Open the door."

He heard soft footsteps, and the handle turned. What he saw, surprised him. He was prepared for tears and heartbreak, not this.

Mary's eyes narrowed on him and seared through him like a sharp sword. There was fire behind her eyes and an odd glint Gunther recognized as only one thing. She wanted to murder him. She'd been angry before, but this was far worse. His death was her only objective. He took a step back and whined like a scared dog. "Mar-eeee," he pleaded. "Come now. Let's talk this out."

"You. I hate you," she growled. "You despicable, worthless piece of rotting flesh." Her voice escalated. She stepped forward, and he kept the distance by walking backward.

He put his hands up. "Now, Mary. Listen to me."

"What's going on?" He heard Anton's voice from behind him.

"Never have I met such a cruel, heartless person," Mary said, ignoring her brother. "If I lived to be a hundred years old, I would never want to meet the likes of you again. You deserve to die!" She picked up a vase of flowers and tried to throw it at him.

Blake dodged and the vase shattered. "Mary!" he yelled. "Get a hold of yourself. If you'll just listen for one minute . . ."

She growled again and then flew at him, hitting and kicking.

He wrestled her arms, trying to pin her down. Anton came from behind and pulled Mary away by her midsection.

"Stop it, Mary!" Anton yelled. Anton never yelled.

Mary did stop then. She sank against Anton and covered her face as sobs escaped. Then she turned and hugged Anton as she cried.

Anton's face revealed the shock Blake felt. Then Anton's eyes pinned him with an accusing glare. "What's going on, Gunther?"

"It's not what you think." Blake stepped closer, but Anton put out his hand. "Come now, Anton. At least hear me out."

"Fine, but I will not force Mary to listen. I want you to leave, Blake. I will ride out when Mary is feeling better."

Blake shook his head. "I'm not leaving. I care about Mary just as much as you, maybe more."

"The difference is, she doesn't care for you. Look at what happened here."

The flowers and glass on the floor, the sound of her cries. Blake felt like he had been gut-punched. He nearly doubled over with pain. Was this what it felt like to love someone so much it hurt? He thought love was supposed to be sunshine and roses.

"Mary, please. This isn't about the money. My mother thinks I'm a rake, but I promise it isn't true. I'll prove it to you. I will. I'll keep begging for your forgiveness from now until eternity."

The cries did not lessen. Anton glowered, and Blake finally pulled himself away.

Chapter Fourteen

A maid brought three letters to Mary's room the next day. The first in the small stack was from her mother. Her tears had barely dried after a long night of heartache. She couldn't bear to read it if it meant bad news. The children's sweet faces came to her mind, spurring her from her bed. She ran to find Anton.

She flew into his office without knocking. She'd never knocked when it had belonged to her father, either. The letter practically flew out of her grasp as she shoved it toward him.

"It's from Mama. I can't open it."

Anton refrained from commenting about her swollen eyes and took the letter. He picked up his penknife and sliced away the wax seal.

He scanned the letter, and his composure relaxed. "Jillian is recovering. Mother should be home by the end of the week."

Mary sank into the seat opposite her brother's desk and squeezed her eyes shut. "I couldn't have survived losing Jillian."

"I know," Anton said. "And God knows. Praise be to Him for getting Jillian through this."

"Amen," Mary said, wiping a stray tear from her eye. She wasn't the only one missing Father right now and counting her blessings she would not have to say goodbye to her sister. She reached forward and took the letter back. "It says to not forget about the Johnsons' ball, as she will likely not be home in time to join us. I admit, I had forgotten."

"Yes, the ball is an oversight with all the angst this family is experiencing. Let me tell the children the good news; I'm afraid your tears will just upset them." Anton stood and moved toward the door.

"Hug them close. I will come up to see them after I take a nap."

She went back to her room and saw the other two letters on the bed. Would one be from Blake with an apology or explanation? She picked up the second and opened it.

It was from Terrance!

The first two paragraphs were surely exaggerated tales of the horrid conditions his estate was in. If they were true, then he and Miss Bliss were in for a great deal of work. It was the third paragraph that caused her to put her hand to her mouth.

Before I left, Anton and I decided to look into the rumors surrounding Gunther. Not out of disloyalty to our friend, and near-brother, but because we hoped uncovering the truth would help you. I did not expect to receive word back from my sources so quickly. As soon as I arrived, a letter met me with a most revealing story. It seems Gunther is beloved by more than just you. Two others, at least, are quite enamored by him. So much so, in fact, that they have tried to outdo each other. They both claimed him as the father to their unborn child in hopes he would be forced to marry one of them. My letter states they have rescinded this claim after a doctor's examination proved both were indeed without child.

I can hardly keep from laughing as I write this. Gunther has never lacked for female attention, but I daresay, I was wrong to jump to conclusions. I do hope he will find this equally amusing when I write to him my apology.

There is more. My farewell dinner enlightened me as to Gunther's feelings for you. I very much believe him to be in earnest in his desire to court you, but I'm worried he will do something out of jealousy. He does not care for Lord Templeton. I will support you in whatever path you choose. Take care of Anton. None of these changes will be easy for him.

Love, Terrance.

Mary stewed for a moment. This cleared up a few concerns but not all. She pulled out the third letter . . . the one with Gunther's seal on the back. She took a steadying breath and then broke the seal with her fingernail.

It wasn't from Blake, but from Mrs. Gunther.

I am writing concerning our little chat the other day. Perhaps I was a bit hasty in my conclusions. I do hope you will forgive me. A mother is apt to think the best and the worst of her child. It is in our nature and cannot be helped.

Mary rolled her eyes. What was she supposed to do now? Believe Blake was a saint? She'd had enough confusing reports to make her feel regretful and frustrated. And where was a letter from Blake? Had he given up on her?

Mary loved a country ball, but tonight she was not in the mood. She sat at her mahogany dressing table in no hurry to leave.

Anton, dressed in his green waistcoat and a fine black evening jacket, leaned against the doorframe of her room. "Lord Templeton will be there."

"I have been ignoring him, so I doubt he will still pay me any heed."

"Come, Mary. I am not thrilled about dancing, but I have to go. Please, don't make me go alone."

Mary sighed and pointed at him with her comb. "You know Blake will be there, and I'm not ready to face him."

"What if he really is innocent in all this?"

"Are you saying he actually loves me?"

"I've never known Gunther to send poetry to anyone. In fact, I've never seen him even read poetry. Come to think on it, can Gunther even read?"

"You've made your point. Some of his efforts do seem sincere, but what about the bargain he made with his mother?"

"So he is supposed to marry someone. Aren't we all? Why not have him choose the person he actually cares for?"

Mary lowered the comb. "Don't make this into something logical. It makes sense when you say it that way, and then my feelings aren't justified. I hardly think that's fair."

Anton looked at her strangely. "Where is Terrance when you need him? He was always better with your problems than me."

Mary dropped her head back against her chair and groaned. "If I could guarantee he loved me and guarantee he would be faithful, I could forgive the bargain debacle."

Anton folded his arms across his chest. "It's become quite clear he loves you. Whether this state lasts or not, I cannot make any promises on his behalf. We all have to decide to trust someone at some point. I trust Blake, but I am not sure I want him to marry my sister. He's already family, so why does he need to marry you, too?"

"Because he and I deserve a chance at something more . . . a family of our own."

Anton's lips quirked upward. "There you have it then. Do you think you have enough faith in him?"

Mary blew out her breath. "I suppose I could observe his behavior at the ball. But don't say anything to him. I should like to see him suffer a little longer."

"Remind me to never fall in love if this is the treatment I expect to receive from my intended."

Mary stuck out her tongue.

Anton chuckled and took a step backward. "You haven't much time so call your maid up, or whatever it is you do to get ready."

She almost laughed at his awkwardness. She couldn't wait to see Anton fall in love. And not with some dream, but with someone who actually returned his affections. Anton deserved to be loved. Her mind drifted to Blake. He deserved to be loved too.

Please, Blake, be the kind of man I can trust!

Mary felt like a criminal under the watchful eye of a constable. No matter where she moved in the ballroom, she felt Blake's eyes follow her. The candlelight and soft music in the dance hall normally created the perfect ambiance, but tonight everything felt off. It was entirely Blake's fault. He'd not danced all night.

This was most unusual for someone who loved to show off his abilities; the man never missed a chance to make an exhibition of himself. He'd not smiled either, and Blake rarely let his true mood show. Not that she was watching him. Well, occasionally she stole a glance over her fan at discreet moments.

"You didn't answer my question, milady."

Mary blinked and registered the man in front of her. She couldn't remember his name. "Forgive me. I am terribly thirsty. I regret that I cannot concentrate on conversation until I have a sip of something."

The man grinned. "Please, let me serve you. I will be but a moment." He hurried off toward the refreshments.

Where was Anton? She searched the room and finally spied him talking to a few matrons. As both an earl and a bachelor, he never lacked attention. However, Anton was the picture of perfect manners and was usually stuck in tiresome conversation and forced to suffer through every outing in company.

She moved across the long, rectangular room and wormed her way through the matrons. "Brother, dear. Might I have a private word?"

Anton's shoulders seemed to droop with relief. He took Mary's arm and they talked themselves through several excuses as they pulled away from the biddies.

"You couldn't have managed that favor before the last set? I could barely breathe with the way they were throwing their daughters at me."

Mary couldn't even bring herself to laugh at him. "Sorry, I was dancing. Have you spoken with Blake?"

"Mr. Gunther?" Anton corrected.

"Oh, stop. Mama isn't here, so there's no need to be ridiculous." Mary put her hands on her hips. "Well, have you?"

Anton shook his head and then started to look for him.

"Don't look now! He'll know we are talking about him."

"I only spoke briefly with him, but it wasn't about you, and it wasn't good."

Mary scrunched her brow. "What do you mean by *it wasn't good*? I've never seen him so miserable."

"That's because he plans to join a convent and become a nun."

Mary snorted. "Be serious. What did he say?"

"It might as well be the truth." Anton sighed. "He's leaving town to visit his aunt. He says he will depart soon and has no idea when he should return."

Mary stood stock still for a moment, processing the shock. Then she huffed. "So why did he come then? To torment me?"

"I don't know, but I aim to find out. Blake Gunther is my closest friend. First Terrance, and now Gunther leaves. I wish you would have broken a different man. Gunther keeps me from taking life too seriously. And after talking to those biddies, I am sure I shall go mad without his company."

Mary folded her arms across her chest. "Remember, it was he who broke my heart, not the other way around. Does the cad plan to at least come say goodbye?"

Anton shrugged, and then his eyes widened. "You could ask him. He's right behind you."

Mary whirled around. Her tongue felt stuck in her mouth. Blake's usually perfectly fluffed chestnut hair seemed flat, and his cravat was rumpled. He stared at her with the same gloomy large brown eyes as Anton's dog. It hurt to see him depressed, but at the same time, she could feel her anger building. Why should he be sad? Mary was the one who was hurt! This could never work. Blake was running away, but didn't he want to fight for her?

Anton cleared his throat. "The silence is killing me. Can you two just kiss and make up already?"

Mary's cheeks burned, and Blake's eyes widened.

Blake coughed into his hand. "I'm afraid that would be the last thing Lady Mary would ever desire." Mary couldn't meet Blake's gaze. "I, uh, just wanted to say goodbye. I plan to ride out in the morning."

Mary still could not make her eyes look up. She was afraid if she did, she'd bawl like a baby. She reached back and subtly grabbed a hold of Anton's arm for support.

"Gunther, you don't have to leave. I understand this is a mess, but can't we talk about this tomorrow? I'll come see you after breakfast."

"I think it's better this way," Gunther said. "Excuse me."

Mary saw his feet shuffle away. When she finally lifted her eyes, it was to see Lord Templeton approaching them.

His gaze followed Blake's retreating form too. "I know you're family friends, but I've heard enough rumors about that man to make me sick. If I were you, Lady Mary, I would steer clear of Mr. Gunther."

Mary's hands fisted. "I didn't know you listened to gossip, Lord Templeton."

"Then you don't believe him capable of ruining the lives of innocent women?"

"He is a harmless flirt and no more," Mary said, shocked how quickly a few rumors had turned into outright slander.

"I apologize. I stand corrected."

Mary glowered at him. "I will accept your apology on behalf of my future husband."

Lord Templeton's surprise would have made her laugh, but she was in too much of a dither. She needed to hurry if she was going to catch Blake.

. She turned and nearly ran into the gentleman, who's name she had forgotten, holding her drink.

He grinned like he'd just found a prize. "There you are. I thought I'd lost you."

Mary couldn't think of anything to say, still flustered by the news of Blake leaving town. "I . . . I . . . Excuse me." She picked up her skirts and hurried from the room, hoping to catch Blake. The corridor was empty, so she gathered her cloak and hurried outside. Why did she feel cold when it was a warm summer evening? Where was Blake?

"Mr. Gunther!" she yelled, rushing down the line of carriages. Blake would have arrived on a horse and not with his parents, so she moved toward the stables. "Blake!" she yelled again, not caring that several footmen and coachman stared at her strangely.

She finally stopped to catch her breath. With Blake gone, there was no reason to return to the party. She found her own family carriage and told the coachman to take her home. He would have to return for Anton, but she was too devastated to care about the inconvenience she was causing.

The ride echoed her loneliness. No one was there to tease her into a smile or commiserate with her. She had dug her own grave by ruining her chances with Lord Templeton. Surprisingly, she didn't even feel guilty about it. Being buried alive would be preferable to life without Blake.

Mary let the footman help her down, but she kept her chin tucked down to hide her tear-streaked face. She ran inside and up the castle's main staircase. Instead of heading to her room, she stopped at her alcove and slipped inside. Her seashell collection caught her eyes first, glowing in the moonlight. Each shell held a memory of Blake. Her sketchbook lay on her chair, and she scooped it up. She wanted to sketch Blake's portrait before she went to bed. There was something comforting about drawing the familiar lines of a loved one. It made them come alive. Not as wonderful as the real thing, but it would be as close as she could get.

She hugged the sketchbook and curled up in her chair. The darkness preyed on her melancholy, and tears coursed down her face. If only she had been more trusting when she had had the chance. If only she had taken a leap of faith.

Footsteps sounded on the stairs, and she held her breath. She chastised herself for not waiting to cry until she was in the privacy of her bedroom. A hiccup escaped, and she slammed her hand over her mouth.

"Is someone there?"

Mary dropped her hand and leaned forward. That voice sounded remarkably like Blake's. Was he here? Mary sucked in her breath and another hiccup escaped—this one far louder than the first.

"Mary?"

Before she could answer, a scrape of metal on the floor pierced the otherwise quiet corridor. The armor moved aside, and Blake filled the space, his face glowing in the moonlight. "Still playing back here after all these years?"

He looked unreasonably happy for someone who should have a broken heart. Embarrassed and frustrated, she sniffed loudly and used her sleeve to wipe her face.

"Mary? What the devil is wrong?"

His shoulders were too broad to squeeze by so he had to shift the armor farther to the side.

"Don't you dare come in here, Blake Gunther!"

Blake didn't listen to her. His large form crowded into her alcove. A small light from the corridor filtered into their space, allowing Mary to better see Blake's confident smile.

"So when is the wedding?"

Mary scowled. "What wedding?"

"You told Lord Templeton I was to be your future husband."

The blood drained from her face. "You heard that? Why, that's impossible!"

"Anton found me and told me, actually."

"But how? You left. I went looking for you."

He squatted down by her. "You did?" His voice was soft.

Mary dropped her gaze and stared at the binding of her sketchbook.

Blake reached forward and lifted her chin. He leaned close, and she could hardly breathe. "I hadn't left yet. My mother stopped to lecture me for not dancing. As soon I removed myself from her clutches, Anton waylaid me. He told me what you said. I had hoped you'd received Terrance's and my mother's letters and you would forgive me, but then you seemed intent on avoiding me tonight."

"You never approached me," Mary explained. "All week, there was nary a word from you. I thought you'd given up on me."

"I wasn't going to leave forever. Just however long it took for you to trust me again. I can't give up on the idea of us. It's all I can think about." His eyes seemed to catch on something. "The cockleshells I gave you as a boy!" He reached over her and picked one up. "You saved these after all these years?"

Mary shrugged, then hiccupped again, and they both laughed. "No matter my complaints, you have always been more than kind to me. Things were simpler when we were children. I fear I've complicated everything."

Blake put his hand on her shoulder and trailed it down the side of her arm. "I know a quick way to uncomplicate things."

"How?" Mary asked, her voice betraying the yearning she felt.

Blake removed the sketchbook from her hands and set it on the floor. Then he helped her to stand. She looked up into his eyes as his hands softly encircled her waist.

"Lady Mary, may I have the honor of a kiss?"

There was hesitancy in his voice. She sensed that if she said no, he would respect her wish and wait however long it took until she was ready. But she was ready now. She leaned into him, closing the small space between them. His hands tightened around her like a gentle hug.

This was it. The moment she'd dreamed about all her life. She stepped on her tiptoes bringing her mouth level with his. A smile touched his lips just before she did. Her arms found his neck, and she returned his embrace. For the next few moments, the man of her dreams was all hers and she was all his.

Their tender kiss deepened, opening the gates of trust. His hands cradled her against him, and the only desire she had was to make him happy. One of them laughed, or maybe it was both of them. They pulled back and grinned at each other.

"You are definitely not a little girl anymore," Gunther whispered. She fisted her hand to whack his arm, but he stopped her. "I'm teasing. I never should have taught you how to box."

Mary wrapped her arms around his middle. "It is a skill I will need if we are to be married."

"A skill you will put to good use when you tire of me as my parents have."

Mary shook her head. "I might be younger than you, Blake Gunther, but I know something you don't. I will never be tired of being in love with you. I might grow annoyed or get angry, but my love for you is so deeply rooted, it cannot be removed."

Blake did something then that she had never seen him do before. His eyes welled up with tears and a drop escaped. "I never believed anyone could love me this way."

Mary wiped away his tear with her thumb. "Well, I do."

Blake captured her hand and kissed it, then traded her hand for her mouth. This time, his lips were fierce against hers and filled with a pledge of enduring love.

A noise sounded behind them, and Anton pulled Gunther back.

"Looks like you followed my advice and fixed things with a kiss," Anton said with wink. "Now it's time for our Romeo to go home."

"Listen," Blake said. "Since we are soon to be officially family, might you do your future brother a favor and go away?"

Anton slapped him on the back. "You've got two minutes, and then I think you and I should have a word in my office."

Blake saluted him and then turned back and reached for Mary's hand. She clasped his and relished the warmth there. "Where were we? Oh, yes. Lady Mary, you have made me the happiest of men. I promise to love you forever."

Mary grinned. "And I promise to never be contrary about one thing . . . my love for you."

Chapter Fifteen

Mary stood next to Blake in front of both of their families. The Gunthers sat on one side of Banbury Castle's drawing room, and Lady Crawford and Anton sat on the other. The surprise family conference had been met with a variety of reactions. Mrs. Gunther's expression was wary, and Mr. Gunther, who sat a foot away from her, was calm. The distance between them seemed measured by their differing expectations for this meeting, and that alone bred further tension. Mary watched her mother steal a concerned glance toward Mrs. Gunther and then to Anton. At least Anton was mostly relaxed.

It was time to tell them.

Blake cleared his throat, and Mary held her breath as he said, "Lady Crawford, Father, Mother . . . Lady Mary and I are going to be married."

Mrs. Gunther clutched her throat, rattling her single strand of pearls. Her gaze pinned Mary to her spot. "Are you sure? Are you really sure?"

Mary swallowed. "Yes, Mrs. Gunther."

She looked to her own mother, who had arrived home from her trip only moments before.

She was not as surprised, just concerned.

"Has something happened while I was away?"

"Just some kissing," Anton said with a smug smile.

Mrs. Gunther gasped. "Forgive my son, Lady Crawford. I am thoroughly ashamed of his behavior."

"Nothing shocking happened," Mary said, stepping toward her mother.

Blake stepped forward too and took Mary's hand. He gave her an encouraging glance. "I fell in love with your daughter, Lady Crawford. We beg your blessing on our union."

After a moment of blustered sputtering from Lady Crawford, Anton interrupted. "You are both butchering this. Mama, we have long been aware of Mary's feelings. I have spoken with them both and believe Gunther to be in earnest. I will vouch for his feelings."

Mother shook her head. "You cannot vouch for someone's love." She turned to Blake. "Dear, I have cared for you like my own son. But I cannot agree to this without a promise that you will love and cherish my daughter for the rest of your life."

Blake leaned close to Mary. "Everyone keeps questioning the fervor of my love for you. Please, do not be offended, my sweet."

Mary glared at him. "Focus."

Mrs. Gunther sighed. "Are you sure, Lady Mary? Completely sure?"

Blake straightened. "Listen, you may sever all my limbs if Mary, here, even begins to question my fidelity. I will never kiss another woman as long as I live. Except you, Mother." He blew out his breath, and Mary could tell he was extremely flustered. He tried again. "I've been searching for happiness in all the wrong places, but through Mary, I've seen a glimpse of what true joy can be. My perspective has changed, as has my heart."

Mary squeezed his hand, reveling in the comfort it brought her. "I couldn't love Blake so much as I do if I did not trust him. I have faith in him and in us." She turned to face him. "I am very sure. He is the only man for me."

Blake's smile was a mixture of relief and pure, unfettered joy. He leaned in to kiss her when Anton coughed. Blake sprung back.

Lady Crawford put her hands together. "This is what I have long hoped for. Finally!"

"What?" Anton leaned forward in his seat. "You do realize that we can never get rid of him again? He will be family. Family is permanent."

"Wait." Blake shook his head. "Are you trying to talk her into this, or out of this?"

"I'm just making sure *she* is sure," Anton said. "And I am also a little annoyed that she acted as if she wasn't going to approve and then suddenly said she does."

"Mothers have hearts too, dear," Mother said. "We are just fiercely protective of our children."

Mary could breathe fully again. "Thank you, Mama."

Both her and Blake turned to Mr. and Mrs. Gunther.

"We ought not to rush into anything," Mrs. Gunther began.

Mr. Gunther put his hand on his wife's, which caused him to nearly fall across the sofa to reach her. "Don't speak, just nod."

Mrs. Gunther's eyes bulged. Her husband never interrupted her. "I . . . you . . ." she stopped and appealed to Lady Crawford. "If you think this is a good idea, then surely I should rely on your superior judgment."

Lady Crawford gave Mrs. Gunther an encouraging smile.

"Aha!" Blake said, pointing at his mother. "Now you must concur."

"We do, son," his father said. "Don't we, Mrs. Gunther?"

She sighed. "I suppose."

Blake pressed his eyes closed, and a smile surfaced on his mouth. He turned and circled his arms around Mary. "You're mine now. And I have a mind to celebrate. There is no escaping this, darling." He dipped her across his leg and nearly smothered her with kisses.

Mary heard Mrs. Gunther squeal and her mother gasp, but all she cared about was the man holding her. Love was worth waiting for.

THE END

Author's Note

Who was the real Lady Mary Contrary? As with most nursery rhymes, there is usually more than one interpretation. Most historians speculate between Mary I, Mary Queen of Scots, and Mary, the mother of Jesus. The symbolism behind the rhyme is often construed as dark, or even bloody, but I chose to offer a lighter rendition.

Another piece of history woven into this tale is Banbury Castle. It originally had two defense ditches (moats), one around the castle keep and one around the castle's defensive wall. It was brought to its knees during the English Civil War and rendered unlivable. This story is set as if the earl's family purchased Banbury Castle and restored it from a medieval fortification to a more modern, late eighteenth century/early nineteenth century structure (without the double moats and leaving a remnant of the wall around the surrounding land). Today it is nothing more than history and a mark on Castle Street, but its stones were used to build up the town around it, which is special in its own way.

About the Author

Anneka Walker is an award-winning author. She was raised by a librarian and an English teacher turned judge. After being fed a steady diet of books, she decided to learn about writing. The result was a bachelor's degree in English and History. When she isn't dreaming up a happy ending for a story, she's busy living her own together with her husband and adorable children.

Anneka also publishes Historical Fiction Romance through Covenant Communications.

Go to **www.annekawalker.com** to sign up for her newsletter or follow her on social media.

Made in the USA
Coppell, TX
16 March 2021

51825224R00094